THAW

ANNIINA SJÖBLOM

Quills & Quartos
PUBLISHING

Edited by Marcelle Wong and Debbie Brown

Cover Design by Ellen J Pickels

Couple walking through the snow, by Anna Whelan Betts, c.1900

ISBN: 978-1-951033-22-4 (ebook) and 978-1-951033-23-1 (paperback)

To Dad, who never read Austen but, like Jane, was a great proficient when it came to dry wit, and always made me laugh.

TABLE OF CONTENTS

This is a most unfortunate affair, and will probably be much talked of

Miss Mary Bennet
Pride & Prejudice Chapter 47

PROLOGUE

Darcy House, Grosvenor Square, December 25, 1811

My dearest Jane,

I am deeply sorry that I have taken so long to respond to the letter you sent after the wedding. I know how much you must have worried for me, but I fear my thoughts have been so heavy of late that I did not know what to write. Can you imagine it was only a month ago that our greatest cause for anxiety was acquiring the shoe-roses for Mr Bingley's planned ball at Netherfield by proxy because of the rain? How long ago that seems; how frivolous such concerns!

I am sorry that you never got to dance with Mr Bingley at his ball. I know how much you expected it. I am sure you will tell me not to be vexed over such little things—but I must. Every moment spent thinking of small concerns is a respite from grieving over the much, much more dire events that have unfolded of late. And dear Jane, apart from a few, fleeting moments, they are all that I think about.

I have not slept. It is Christmas, but I have not eaten. I fear I have quite forgotten how to smile. But I suppose it is of no matter—I expect my future will have very few moments in store for me to use such an expression. I know it is not what you want to hear, and you know it is not in my nature to say such things lightly, but say it I must: I think I rather hate my husband. It is with great solemnity and not an ounce of levity that I declare I would rather have married Mr Collins. He is a fool, to be sure, but I would rather be the wife of a fool than of a man like Mr Darcy. My husband.

A week ago, when I embraced you after the wedding breakfast for one last time before starting the journey to London, I was prepared to accept my fate with as much a semblance of grace as I could muster. My husband and I did not talk much on the way, apart from some rather insignificant remarks on the weather and what I was to expect when we arrived in London. He described the house to me, pointing out such things as the number of servants and the size of the rooms—all told with such a watchful eye that I was at a loss to understand what sort of a reaction he was expecting. Was I supposed to be pleased at the prospect of being mistress of such a house? Or would he have disapproved of me even more if I looked too eager to hear it all? Quite tired and rather wishing to avoid any sort of an argument, I did my best to refrain from showing any emotion and only nodded every once in a while to give the impression that I was paying attention.

But the evening of the day showed me how perfectly useless all my earlier efforts were to avoid a disagreement. Oh Jane! I do not know if I should tell you this, but I much fear that, if I do not say it to someone, I might lose my mind. Certainly, in the past days I have been able to think of little else.

After we sat through an awkward dinner, exchanging polite nothings under the near-constant scrutiny of the rather intimidating butler and the footmen serving the food, we were left to our own devices. It was then that my husband decided it was time to educate me on his views of our current situation. It has been a week, and I still cannot quite grasp what happened.

For almost half an hour, he paced back and forth in the room, speaking eloquently and with great feeling of his misfortunes and what a great sacrifice he had made by condescending to wed me. It seems that having a wife such as myself is a degradation, the magnitude of which I could not possibly understand. All the benefits of our union, it seems, must be on my side. My faults can hardly be counted—every single thing, from the professions of our uncles to the supposedly indifferent education we have received, speaks against me. Our relations—even our very own family—are such that he would not wish to recognise the connexion. Not to speak of the good people of Meryton, amongst whom there is not even a shred of civility to be found.

After everything that has happened in the past month, I found this last assertion to be something I can almost agree with. I do not hold very fond feelings towards our friends and neighbours after the ignoble way they have treated me. But the rest of his speech left me in such a state of shock, I was at first quite speechless. Oh Jane! It seems my husband took my silence for something quite different than it was. When he had finished his soliloquy, he approached me with an odd look in his eyes, obviously still quite agitated from his heated speech. He stopped, he breathed—and then, quite unexpectedly, bent down in what I can only assume was an attempt to kiss me.

It was then that I regained my wits. I can hardly believe he thought that after such a speech I would ever allow for such liberties! Can you? I pushed him away and told him that he forgot himself—and of what happened then, perhaps the less said the better. I told him in no uncertain terms exactly how little impressed I am with his wealth and consequence. I expressed, with very great energy, my wish that he had never set foot in Hertfordshire and that I could take back every event that led to our unfortunate union.

By the time I was done, it was his turn to be at a loss for words—and thank goodness for that! I do not think I could have suffered another minute of that conversation. For a moment, he just stood and stared at me. Then he bowed and said that he understood my feelings perfectly—and left the room.

It has been a week and we have barely spoken since. He seems as determined to avoid me as I am to avoid him, and I am starting to understand the benefits of having such a large house and so many servants to assure that, even when our paths do cross, we are rarely alone.

Oh Jane! I am sorry to burden you so, but I cannot help it. How I wish it were all just a figment of my imagination—a fearsome dream I could laugh at when I awake in the morning! But it is not. And I do not understand how I can ever make peace with all that has happened.

Let other pens dwell on joy and happiness. I fear mine has quite lost the ability.

Your loving sister,

~~E.B.~~

E.D.

CHAPTER ONE

A Discourteous Man from Derbyshire

Longbourn, October 7, 1811

My dearest Aunt,

You have asked me to tell you something diverting. I am happy to report that your request has come at quite an opportune time and I can oblige with no great trouble: the new occupant of Netherfield Park has arrived at last!

I must say that I feel sorry for the poor fellow already. His chaise and four has barely entered the neighbourhood, and already there is such talk of matrimony that one should think an Indian maharaja has arrived in a caravan of fifty elephants, ready to choose a shocking number of Hertfordshire wives to take back with him across the perilous seas.

Papa has met our mysterious new neighbour, Mr Bingley, twice now, but he is perfectly unreliable when it comes to describing his looks or character. Lady Lucas told us in church yesterday that he is *wonderfully* handsome and *extremely* agreeable, which seems rather promising, do you not agree? Mr Bingley himself did not make an appearance at church, which has left poor Mary gravely concerned for his character.

I am sure you remember Mr John Powlett, the Meryton tradesman with whom Uncle has done business on occasion? To our surprise, he has proposed to our Frances at the fair last week and it looks likely that we will have to find a new maid soon. I would not go as far as to say that the frock I gave her had something to do with the matter, but I daresay she looked extremely pretty in it. Mama is rather disgruntled. She has expressly instructed me that I am not to give any of my old garments to servants in the future, lest they all abandon us to fend for ourselves.

Mama, Lydia, and Kitty are spending the day with Aunt Philips, and Papa is gone to resolve a dispute between John Thompson and Martin Baker. For the first time in weeks, I have the sitting room all to myself—and, obliging niece that I am, I have chosen to spend my quiet time by writing to you!

As I am sure that Papa's tenants are not of first and foremost interest to you, I shall spare you the details of the quarrel between Thompson and Baker. Suffice it to say that it involves a mutinous cow, a broken fence, and a rather fine counterpane that Polly Thompson had inherited from her great-grandmother. I would not much care for the whole debacle if I did not know that Mrs Hill has made a somewhat unfortunate proposal to Papa on how to appease the Thompsons: she thinks it might soothe their shaken sensibilities if Papa offered their oldest daughter Lettice the opportunity to take over for our dear Frances.

It is a prospect I do not anticipate so much. Much like Mama, it seems that Lettice Thompson blames me for Mr Powlett's decision to propose to our Frances. According to Charlotte Lucas, Lettice had harboured hopes of receiving a similar offer from Mr Powlett herself. Poor John Powlett, to have people give so little credit to the steadfastness of his heart as to think he would make such a decision solely over a pretty frock!

I am not overly concerned, though, for I am convinced that very little can be resolved at all. Baker and Thompson are known to quarrel over every insignificant matter, and I find it unlikely that Papa would go to any great lengths to solve this particular altercation. At least, he has rarely done so before.

I was very pleased to hear that Uncle will not need to travel, after all. Does that mean we can rekindle our hopes of having you here with us for Christmas? Nothing would please me more!

And of course, you must tell me—did Miss Harding wear feathers or fruit on her bonnet when last you saw her? You know my younger sisters well enough to understand that I shall not have a moment's peace until I find out the answer.

Remember me fondly to Uncle and the children—especially to the children, for I find them more likely to forget me.

Your loving niece,

E.B.

Longbourn, October 17, 1811

My dearest Aunt,

You will forgive me for taking so long to reply to your last when I tell you that it was all done for a very good purpose. If I had written any earlier, I would not have been able to give you the first-hand description of our new neighbour and his illustrious companions that you are now about to receive!

There was a ball in Meryton two evenings ago. I wore my yellow muslin, with the trimmings refashioned as you suggested. Charlotte Lucas, at least, was of the opinion that it was quite a success.

(Some of the attendants might not have agreed with her, but you will have to wait a while to find out more!)

Mr Bingley arrived at the ball with a party of four, a little later than most but not so much as to appear uncivil. I was wrong to doubt the accuracy of the reports we received earlier from Lady Lucas. Mr Bingley's manners were every bit as pleasing as has been suggested. He was amiable and unreserved, polite and unaffected, and made it the pursuit of his evening to acquaint himself with the people present.

Towards the close of the ball, Charlotte overheard him tell Mr Robinson quite decidedly that he thought Jane was beyond a doubt the prettiest lady in the room. Who could but be charmed by such obvious good sense and incomparable judgment?

At the ball with Mr Bingley were his two sisters, the husband of the elder sister, and a rather discourteous young man from Derbyshire whom it would please me to never meet again. Mr Bingley's sisters were elegant in that uninviting manner some people have of being rather too aware of their own elegance to truly deserve the word. And if the sisters were not altogether impressed by their present society, Mr Bingley's friend Mr Darcy was even less so. A gentleman of some standing, he made very little by way of effort to conceal his distaste for the company of anyone outside his own party.

Mr Bingley made the grave mistake at one point of trying to induce him to dance, and I made the even graver mistake of overhearing his reply to this entreaty—for it was myself that Mr Bingley proposed to him as a partner. I would encourage you to guess what happened next, but I flatter myself enough to think that you never could conceive of such a scene! He turned, he looked—and declared me to be tolerable at most, obviously slighted by other men, and certainly nothing at all to tempt him.

You know I am not a vain creature by nature, but being so described has left me with no very cordial feelings towards his person. That he hails from Derbyshire, a county I have heard you speak of so often and so fondly, must remain his sole redeeming quality!

With this shocking tale, I shall leave you, for Lydia and Kitty have entreated me this half an hour to walk with them to Meryton. Give my love, etc. to Uncle and the children.

Your tolerable niece,

E.B.

Longbourn, November 1, 1811

My dearest Aunt,

What a sweet creature you are, to come so valiantly to my defence! While I can say with certainty that there was not a single sickly, miserable spinster in sight to confuse me with, the idea has amused me greatly! But I am determined to think on it no more. Mr Darcy is free to dislike me as much as he chooses, if it gives him pleasure. He seems like the sort of fellow who has very little pleasure in anything at all, and I therefore presume that this tiny morsel of it might be of some use to him.

I read your latest letter aloud one evening after supper and, as it has proved an enduring topic of conversation, I feel it my duty to report to you the manifold thoughts it has raised in the members of our family. A few of the passages I did reserve for Jane's ears alone, as I felt that you had likely not intended them for an evening's entertainment.

Papa was so enthusiastic to hear that Uncle had procured a copy of *Meditations* with Coleridge's scribblings on it, he said he had half a mind to write to Uncle and ask if he could perchance borrow such a treasure. As I know, however, it is the other half of his mind which often prevails when it comes to the business of letter-writing, I take it upon myself to ask that you mention this to Uncle.

Lydia and Kitty have occupied themselves chiefly with bugle

beads after I read them the letter. I have feared such a development ever since I saw how they fawned over Miss Bingley's headdress when we dined at Lucas Lodge last week, and now your description of Miss Harding's reticule has confirmed it—suddenly, nothing can be quite fashionable without a trim of bugle beads. As for myself, anyone may know how I detest the odious little things and much prefer ribbon any day of the week.

Though she is very demure about it, Jane was visibly pleased by your supposition of Mr Bingley already being in love with her. I do not think that four dances and a few short meetings are quite sufficient for anyone with sense to form a lasting attachment, but Mr Bingley's marked attentions to Jane are almost enough to make me question these formerly firm beliefs. Charlotte is of the opinion that Jane, too, should be more open and determined in her displays of affection—she talks about 'fixing' him! What a ghastly word!

Frances and Mr Powlett are to be married tomorrow morning, and she will leave us immediately. Mama still considers it a monstrous betrayal, even though the new maid will start in a few days and, between Mrs Hill and Sarah, I doubt it will take her very long at all to settle in. I am happy to report that the events I feared earlier did not transpire—Papa did not employ Lettice Thompson, and I am saved from the looming threat of an accidental tear in a favourite dress at the hands of a jilted maid.

Give my love, etc. to Uncle and the children (and do tell Edward he need not worry, as we most definitely will have plum cake on Christmas—it is my favourite, too!).

Your affectionate niece,

E.B.

Netherfield, November 15, 1811

My dearest Aunt,

I am writing to you from the confines of one of the guest bedrooms in Netherfield. Jane has fallen ill during a visit to Miss Bingley and her sister, and we are under orders from the apothecary not to move her until she is feeling better. Do not be alarmed—it is a rather violent cold, but Mr Jones has assured us that there is no great cause for worry.

I arrived here two days ago after Jane sent us a note explaining that she was unwell. I found her weak and feverish, but quite well cared for. Mr Bingley's sisters are remarkably adept at forgetting all about her when they are not in her immediate presence but, when they do attend to her, they do so with at least the appearance of affection and solicitude. The only thing the sisters lack in their efforts is sincerity; thankfully, their brother has an ample supply of it to make up for this deficiency.

The more I see of Mr Bingley, the better I like him. His might not be the most intricate of characters, but there is something quite beguiling about the transparent manner in which he expresses himself. When he says that he is full of concern for Jane's well-being, there can be no doubt of his meaning exactly what he says. In his eagerness to please her, he encouraged me to choose any book from his library to read aloud to Jane during her waking hours. You know well my fondness for spying on other people's libraries, so you can imagine how pleased I was with the prospect!

I admit, however, that my enthusiasm was dampened somewhat as I entered the library. Not because the collection of books was quite meagre—which it was (but Mr Bingley is such an amiable man that I find it difficult to hold against him the fact that he is clearly not a great reader)—rather, it was because his odious friend Mr Darcy had chosen that exact same moment to occupy the library. He barely noted my arrival, so I determined to ignore him to the best of my ability. Oh, Aunt. It has only been a short acquaintance, but I cannot tell you how much I detest the man!

While he did not say a word, I could easily detect that he was staring at me whenever he thought I would not notice. It has been his exasperating habit of late to hover about, staring at me with a satirical eye but not uttering a word if he can help it. I do not understand what he means by it. He has already declared me tolerable—surely there is no need to always be investigating the matter for further proof of my faults!

My vanity told me to choose the most serious, tedious tome available to assure that I would offer him no further cause for reproof to add to my undoubtedly long list of deficiencies. But, as I am sure you can guess, my impertinence led me in another direction entirely. With some pride, I confess that I chose the most shocking novel I could find (from Miss Bingley's personal collection, I have no doubt!) and, as innocently as I could muster, asked whether he had perchance read it. Oh, how I wish that you could have seen his reaction! His eyes widened in shock at my presumption, and the corners of his mouth turned down in such contempt that I found it very, very hard not to laugh. I must say, I have never heard anyone say 'Most certainly not' with such a great emphasis!

Of course, the episode cannot but make me sink further in his estimation. But I do not much care—let him despise me to bide his time in the country!

I shall close now, for Jane has awakened and requires my attention. I much expect to entice a smile out of her with a description of my encounter in the library.

We both send all our love and impatient wishes of seeing you, Uncle, and the children. I shall write to you again in a few days to let you know how Jane's condition has improved.

Yours in affection,

E.B.

Longbourn, November 17, 1811

My dearest Aunt,

I am happy to report that Jane has recovered almost entirely, and we are again back at home where we belong. Mama, while happy that Jane is recuperating, is most displeased with me for having arranged Mr Bingley's carriage to bring us home today.

I daresay Mr Bingley shares her displeasure at our departure (though he was a great deal more courteous about it), but I cannot be sorry. While our sojourn at Netherfield provided a measure of interesting discoveries about our new neighbours, it would have felt quite unseemly to trespass on their hospitality any longer than was absolutely necessary. I do not care what Mr Bingley's sisters think of me, but I would not have them think ill of Jane.

I believe the timing of our departure might be the first thing Miss Bingley and I have ever agreed upon—and quite possibly the last. I am not altogether sure why she detests me so much, but it has become evident in the past few days that she does. Perhaps it is because I am not suitably impressed by the illustrious Mr Darcy, who is her obvious favourite.

What she sees in him—apart from his wealth—I cannot tell, for he is possibly even more disagreeable towards her than he is to other people. But it seems clear to me that Miss Bingley means to make a husband of Mr Darcy. To be sure, I have never seen such extraordinary determination in a woman. I do not think I ever spent a quarter of an hour in the same room with them without her extolling some supposed virtue of his at least once. I am confident that Charlotte would be proud of her!

Mary has asked me to tell you that she found the book you mentioned earlier from Clarke's library this very morning. She is studiously writing extracts as we speak, so I expect I shall never have to read it myself, as any extract Mary writes is always sure to be read aloud at one point or another. Though Lydia and Kitty have not asked me to mention it, I wish to shock you with the following information: they have also taken to spending a great deal of time at Clarke's of late. Before you start giving them recommendations, however, I must admit that books have very little to do with their newly found fascination with the establishment.

A regiment of the militia has recently arrived in the area and is to remain camped here the whole winter, with Meryton as its head-quarters. Lydia and Kitty have been quite unable to stop talking about the officers. Lest it is absolutely pouring, a daily walk to Meryton has become a fixture in their schedule. I do laud the amount of exercise it provides them, but otherwise I would rather see them occupy their time in some other manner.

At Lydia's behest, Mr Bingley has promised to give a ball at Netherfield once Jane is fully recovered. An exact date has not yet been set, but I do know that white soup will be served and that the host of the evening has advised his surly friend to escape to his rooms before it all begins, should he still find the idea of dancing as intolerable as he has in the past. Miss Bingley, I am sure, will be sorely disappointed if that were to happen!

Papa has been acting uncommonly mysterious and distracted this evening. He has barely teased us at all. If that is not proof enough that something is afoot, he said 'Certainly, my dear' when Lydia asked if she and Kitty could have the coach tomorrow to call upon Aunt Philips if it should happen to rain. Most alarming! I am determined not to give him the pleasure of going to his library to ask about it, only to have him give some vague, teasing reply—whatever great secret he is hiding will surely reveal itself in due course.

I remain, as always, your curious and affectionate niece,

E.B.

Longbourn, November 23, 1811

My dearest Aunt,

Papa's great secret has been revealed—and I would never have made light of it in my last letter had I known it would turn out to be such an acute source of misery! Our cousin Mr Collins has arrived to visit us in a rather queer quest of making amends for the unfortunate fact that he will inherit the entire estate once

Papa passes (an altogether gloomy thought, as I am sure you will agree).

It would be a perfectly laudable pursuit but for one thing: I have been made privy to the fact that he plans to atone for the situation by offering his hand in marriage to one of his fair cousins. And to my utter horror, it seems he has chosen me as the primary recipient of his attentions! Before you jump into a happy consideration of the practical advantages such a match could have, please allow me to describe the gentleman to you in a few words to assist in creating a fuller picture of the situation.

Mr Collins is a clergyman of five and twenty and recently was made rector of a respectably sized parish in Hunsford, Kent. This would be nothing against him were he not also blessed with a mean understanding and absolutely no sense to speak of. To this, he also adds such an odd mixture of servility and self-importance as to render him the most ridiculous, insufferable nincompoop I have ever had the privilege to meet.

For his parish, he owes thanks to a Lady Catherine de Bourgh, to whom he was recommended by a lucky chance just as the living became available. By his description, Lady Catherine is the wisest, most generous, and affable of ladies to ever grace this good earth. I have heard other rather opposite descriptions of her ladyship of late, to which I am prone to put more weight, but more on that later.

As of yet, our cousin has only hinted at his intention of choosing me as the partner of his future life, but it seems probable to me—and more alarmingly, to Mama—that a proposal is soon forthcoming. Oh, Aunt, I do not know what to do! I dread the thought of receiving such a proposal, and doubly so the quarrel that will surely ensue after my refusing it. I can only hope some unexpected happenstance might occur to prevent his asking altogether.

On a happier note: Mr Collins is not the only young man to have recently arrived in the neighbourhood. You will laugh at me when I tell you this, but it is a new officer of the militia that I am speaking of—a Mr Wickham—who has recently taken a commission in the regiment. After only two meetings, I am already quite charmed by him. He has an exceptionally pleasing countenance, a most gentlemanlike manner, and his sound and pleasing conversation has entertained me to an extent I did not think possible.

He has also relayed to me a history (the details of which I shall not put in a letter, as the matter is confidential) that has fully convinced me of my previous estimation of the character of Mr Darcy. Indeed, not only convinced but quite surpassed it, for it seems that he is not only disagreeable but, rather, so devoid of any honour and common decency towards his fellow creatures that it is almost beyond belief.

From Mr Wickham, I have also learned that our cousin's benefactress, Lady Catherine, is the aunt of the despicable Mr Darcy. Mr Wickham describes her as a dictatorial, insolent woman. Her daughter and Mr Darcy are expected to eventually unite their two estates by marriage, leaving our dear friend Miss Bingley sadly in the path of yet another disappointment!

I shall close now, for the incessant rain that has been pestering us since yesterday morning is showing some signs of abating, and I long to go for a walk. I shall write to you again after Mr Bingley's ball, which is set to be held Tuesday next.

Give all my love, etc. to Uncle and especially to my darling little cousins—who must have all my cousinly love, for I wish to reserve none for Mr Collins!

Yours in affection,

E.B.

CHAPTER TWO

Idle Gossip

Longbourn, November 26, 1811

My dearest Aunt,

You will forgive me, I hope, if I do not immediately respond to the questions you had on Mr Collins and Mr Wickham. In my last letter, I expressed a hope that something unexpected would happen to prevent our cousin from proceeding with his awkward attempts at attaining my affection—and now I am much afraid something *has* happened to do exactly that, but at some cost to my own well-being.

After I finished my previous letter to you, I did go for a walk as planned. The rain had not quite abated, but it was only a thin drizzle and I did not consider it a significant impediment. I decided to walk around Mr Thompson's pond, as the path is a favourite of mine and I thought it suitably short in case the skies opened up again. Oh, Aunt. I do believe I might rather have dealt with Mr Collins proposing than with all that happened next.

I was walking down the path on the steeper bank of the pond, when suddenly the ground seemed to disappear from under me. I lost my balance and stumbled downwards—and of what happened then, I am afraid I cannot give you a very clear picture. I was in the water for what surely must have been only a very short moment, but it did not feel like it. And then, quite unexpectedly, I felt someone take hold of me and pull me out of the water.

I beg you not to laugh. It was Mr Darcy. He had apparently been on the far side of the pond with his horse and, when he saw me fall, jumped in the water to rescue me. After he lifted me safely onto the bank, he asked if I was unharmed but, before I even knew the answer myself, he saw that I was not. My spencer had been torn and my shoulder was bleeding quite heavily. It took me a moment to realise how very, very much it hurt.

I confess that I do not yet know what to think of it all. I almost wish I had more of a propensity to faint when in distress so I would not have to think of it at all! Mr Darcy removed my spencer and, having located the wound, tied it with his neckcloth as best he could. Once satisfied that he had done all he could to stop the bleeding, he fetched his coat, wrapped it around me, lifted me up, and proceeded to carry me all the way back to Longbourn.

He did not say much during the entire ordeal, but all he did say and do was done in a respectful, gentlemanly manner, with an efficiency and selflessness that I would not have expected from such a proud man. His horse was abandoned and his fine clothes ruined but, if he gave it a moment's thought, I saw nothing about it. His sole focus seemed to be on assuring my well-being. Considering what I had recently learned of his character, it was all quite remarkable.

Once we reached home, he commanded the situation with such authority that even Mama was quiet and calm for a moment. A servant was sent to fetch the apothecary, and Lydia, who happened to be there when we arrived, was sternly ordered to find me dry clothes. When she started to protest, he silenced her with a look. If I had not been feeling so weak, I might have laughed. It was only after he had left, and I had been put to bed, that the uproar began.

At first, the general commotion revolved around my condition. But Jane tells me that after Mr Jones had visited, examined the wound (which is, fortunately, only a shallow cut accompanied by a mild contusion, and already very much on the mend), and given me a draught to help me sleep, quite a number of other concerns were aired. At the time, I was happily spared from hearing them, but unfortunately the situation seems to have only deteriorated since.

The ball at Netherfield, which was to take place today, has been postponed for now. I am sure you can guess on whom Lydia and Kitty place the fault for this. Mama is distraught over some nonsensical gossip that has reached her ears about what happened. Jane and I have told her not to be, as anyone with an ounce of sense would not give credit to such idle talk. Apparently, however, we do not know how she suffers. I daresay she is right.

Our cousin has learned the identity of my unexpected saviour. He is in high dudgeon because I have acted so heedlessly in front of the nephew of his esteemed patroness. While I am happy this appears to have distracted him from his previous pursuits, I am less pleased that he seems set on driving me quite mad with his endless lectures on propriety. Mary, in what I can only suppose is a most peculiar effort at showing sisterly solicitude, supports him in this endeavour.

After three days, I am utterly fatigued by it all. Apart from Jane and Papa, everyone in this household seems set to despise me. It is almost as if even the servants look at me strangely.

If that were not enough, I suddenly owe a debt of gratitude to the very man I was so determined to detest above all others only a few days ago. And while this man has paid me a call, together with his friend, to ascertain that I am recovering from my fall, there is another young man I would much rather have seen but have not heard a word of.

Do write as soon as you can to tell me what you think of all this. And if you can, tell me something amusing to distract me from my troubles. I am especially looking forward to hearing every detail of your visit to the gardens. Did little Edward carry through his ambitious plan of climbing the many steps to the top of the Chinese Pagoda? And if he did, did he find the view worth his troubles?

You have my affection, always,

E.B.

Longbourn, November 30, 1811

My dearest Aunt,

Thank you for your quick and thoughtful reply. It has consoled me, but only briefly, for it seems that the news I have to relay grows more distressing by the day. I shall try to explain, if I can find it in my power to do so, but I must admit to being so deeply confused, so full of indignation this morning, that I hardly know where to start.

In the past few days, the full extent of the idle gossip I referred to in my previous letter has been revealed to us. As things stand now, I cannot believe it was only four short days ago that I told Mama she was foolish to fret over the things she had heard. At first, it was only some vague references heard by Aunt Philips that something untoward had happened. Then, three days ago, Lydia and Kitty returned from a walk to Meryton quite inconsolable because they had been exceedingly stared at and not at all talked to when they had stopped at Clarke's.

But it was not until Charlotte came to call on us later that same day that I understood something was truly amiss. Dear Aunt, prepare yourself for something that is equal parts dreadful and inconceivable: it seems that, while I was under the impression Mr Darcy saved me, most all of our friends and neighbours seem to be labouring under the idea that he has, in fact, ruined me. Can you believe it? I cannot, but it seems I must.

Little is known as to where the rumours originated, but it appears that someone claims to have witnessed some sort of unseemly, improper behaviour between Mr Darcy and myself. Now the entire neighbourhood is talking about it as if it was a universal truth. It is all so absurd, I try to laugh at it, but I cannot. How can anyone believe such a fabrication? The more I think of it, the more unfathomable it seems. However, even Charlotte thought there might be some truth to what is being said, though I was quick to disabuse her of the notion. It appears there are some details to the story that add credibility. I did not much care to hear what they are.

Mama has taken to her apartment and refuses to come out. She is quite despondent, and I am not sure I can blame her. The focus of her vexation varies from our neighbours—how could they have used us so ill?— to myself. To my endless consternation, she seems to entertain a suspicion every now and then that perhaps I did something improper to cause this after all. It need not be said how very much it offends me.

Though at first he barely seemed to take notice of the matter, pausing only to admire the absurdity of it all, even Papa has grown serious. It is perhaps because our cousin cannot stop talking about it—though he does appear more concerned for the damage any further connexion to us could cause to himself (and, of course, by association, to Lady Catherine de Bourgh) than of the damage to our family. All thoughts of the olive branch he came here to offer are forgotten. It is a blessing, I believe, on both sides that he is leaving us today.

I should wish him gone already, but he refuses to leave until Papa and Mr Darcy emerge from the library. Earlier this morning, against my express wishes (I had hoped that from this one embarrassment, at least, I could be spared), Papa sent a servant to Netherfield with a request for a visit from Mr Darcy. He responded to the summons with unexpected alacrity, arriving with the servant instead of sending a note. After entering the house, he marched directly into the library without a word to any of us. I daresay I have never seen anyone look quite so cross.

More than an hour has now passed since his arrival. I have not been offered the privilege of participating in whatever conversation is taking place between them. The more time passes, the more I dread what is being said. Mr Collins is deeply offended that he has not been included in the discussion. His things have been packed and the horses are ready, but he is pacing stubbornly back and forth in the yard, waiting for the gentlemen in the library to come out. I have been led to understand that he feels duty-bound to give as thorough a report of the situation to his patroness as possible. Insufferable gossip.

Oh, Aunt! I am shocked; I am humiliated. I know it is not quite sound, but I cannot help placing some of the blame for what has happened on Mr Darcy. These people are my friends and neighbours, most of whom I have known all my life. It cannot be on *my* account that someone has seen fit to spread such malicious lies. It is *his* pride and arrogance that everyone is so universally disgusted with. If only he had behaved with more civility towards the society here, then perhaps this could all have been avoided. If only he had left me to my own devices that day. I would rather be at the bottom of Mr Thompson's pond than in the situation I currently find myself in. (Very well, it is an exaggeration. I am not stupid enough to not understand that, whatever his faults, he has done me a kindness. But I cannot help it. And I am sure that he already very much regrets his actions.)

I will end now; if you have read thus far, you have already endured more than your share of this misery. Jane is trying to encourage me to go walking with her in the garden, but I am not sure I am willing to comply. She thinks a little fresh air would serve me well, but who knows what further calamity will befall me if I ever set foot out of this house again?

Your wretched niece,

E.B.

Longbourn, December 2, 1811

My dearest Aunt,

I am to be married.

Your eyes do not deceive you. Married. My every feeling rejects the notion. Yet it is to be.

Having discussed the topic at great length on Saturday with Mr Darcy, my father has determined it is the only solution that can restore any semblance of peace and dignity to the situation. Mr Darcy, to my astonishment, agreed to such an arrangement. I cannot imagine him being anything other than disgusted by the prospect; that he has agreed to it must be attributed to the excessive family pride mentioned by Mr Wickham. He is keen to preserve it at any cost.

Mama is elated. Papa hides in his library. Lydia and Kitty seem to think it all a good joke. Mary has declared me the architect of my own misery. I cannot suffer to even look at any of them.

Oh, Aunt, I am sensible of the evil that would be due to myself and all my sisters were the matter left unresolved. If I remained at Longbourn, I would be a constant reminder of the supposed disgrace to our family. The morning service yesterday was sufficient proof of that. If I were to remove to Gracechurch Street, to stay with you and Uncle for a time, my absence could but add to the already rampant gossip. Marriage seems a dear price to pay for the felicity of those who seem to so little appreciate the sacrifice. For Jane, and Jane alone, I shall do it.

I shall close now. I cannot write. Every word seems to etch the truth of what is about to happen deeper into stone. With such a man as a husband, what is to become of me?

Yours, etc.,

E.B.

CHAPTER THREE

Calico and Cambric

Longbourn, December 6, 1811

My dearest Aunt,

I thank you from the bottom of my weary heart—both for your comforting words and for persuading Mama that a trip to town was wholly unnecessary. I do not know what clever arts you employed to convince her, but I can confirm they were successful. She is now quite settled that the shops in Meryton will do. It is a relief. I appreciate the necessity of purchasing wedding clothes but do not possess the equanimity at present to discuss calico and cambric with her.

Her insistence on extensive farewell visits to the families of the neighbourhood has also abated. I have not the smallest doubt that I have you to thank for it. It is enough that I am forced to stand the poorly concealed curiosity and condescension of Mama's dear friends when they come to call on her. They nod compassionately when we tell them there is not an ounce of truth to the rumours. Even should they believe us, I can see that, in their eyes, the gossip is too tempting, the scandal too delicious to give up.

I do not wish to see any of them and refuse to give them the pleasure of seeing me care about their resentment. Let them triumph over us at a distance and be satisfied. It is they who have injured me and not the other way around. I hope the day will come when they see their misguidance and regret it.

In less than a fortnight, I shall be married. The thought is devastating. A licence will be purchased shortly, and my future husband (how absurd that sounds!) has gone to London to settle the other necessities required. As I am sure you know, Papa has written to Uncle about it. I am grateful for any assistance he can offer on Papa's behalf, should Mr Darcy deign to ask. He is not to return until shortly before the dreaded event, for which I am thankful. I have spoken to him only once since the matter was settled, and it offered me little comfort.

He came to call on us with Mr Bingley two days ago. Miss Bingley and her sister did not choose to join them and were not at all mentioned during the visit, which does not surprise me. They must be livid. Of their brother's steadfast kindness, I am ever grateful. The gentleman were with us scarcely half an hour, but it must have been sufficient to raise within Mr Darcy the deepest regret for having agreed to marry me

At first, the visit was merely extremely uncomfortable. Mr Darcy enquired after the state of my shoulder, to which I replied that it had healed tolerably well. He told me he regretted taking me away from Longbourn so soon but that he and Papa had agreed it would be best to have the matter sorted before Christmas—an absurd notion, as I am sure that any lengthened wait would not make the situation any less regretful to either of us. After that he had little to say but, unfortunately, much to observe.

While somewhat subdued, Mama's delight in the turn events have taken could not but mortify me. She thought only of his wealth. Every word uttered, every thoughtless question asked, seemed to add to the growing look of disapproval and contempt on Mr Darcy's face. Although Jane did her utmost to check them, Lydia's mirth and Kitty's accompaniment did little to improve the situation. Towards the end of the visit, Mr Darcy did not speak at all and merely stared into the distance with a dark look on his face; it was left for Mr Bingley to reply to Mama's queries as best he could.

Mr Wickham and Mr Denny have been to call on us this morning. It was altogether an odd quarter of an hour and, in any other circumstance, would have left me even more unsettled than it did. That Mr Denny was embarrassed and ill at ease, I can well understand. It was clear that he was there at Mr Wickham's behest, and his manner made obvious his wish to be anywhere else but in our drawing room. After their initial joy at seeing the officers arrive had dissipated, Lydia and Kitty were quite put out by his lacklustre efforts at conversation.

Mr Wickham's behaviour was more difficult to comprehend. His manner was cold but seemed to speak less of disappointment and more of something else—though what it was, I cannot quite determine. Perhaps he thought I had misled him when I described my previous dealings with Mr Darcy. But then, he did not seem angry, either. He made some desultory remarks and then, when the attention of others in the room was momentarily elsewhere, asked with some urgency if I had shared with Mr Darcy the details of our previous conversations. I told him I had not. That, Aunt, seemed to entirely serve his purpose of coming, for he rose, said that they had already taken up too much of our morning, and took his leave with a relieved Mr Denny in tow.

I had thought of seeing Mr Wickham and been prepared to explain the entire miserable affair. In my imaginings, he was the one person who would understand my upset at what had happened and be able to commiserate unlike any other—even, perhaps, express some regret on his own behalf, though such thoughts can make little difference now. How foolish I now feel! He expressed no regret; there was not a flicker of sympathy in his looks. His sole concern seemed to be that he had confided in the wrong person. But perhaps it is as well that it should be so. I expect I shall never see him again. His confidences I shall strive to keep, for it can serve no purpose to expose him to any further ill treatment on my future husband's part. But I shall not miss him.

Give all my love, etc. to Uncle and the children, and write to me again as soon as you may.

Your loving niece,

E.B.

Longbourn, December 11, 1811

My dearest Aunt,

However briefly, you have made me laugh. Amidst all the grief and misery of the past weeks, to find that I am still capable of it is a blessing. You know I am not formed for melancholy, but I fear that recent events might have altered my disposition permanently; at the very least, it has been put to a test I should never have wished to experience.

It is true, as you say, that my future husband cuts a fine figure when regarded from a distance (and if I am lucky, and his estate as grand as Miss Bingley describes it, that is how I most often hope to view him). However, I must warn you not to draw any definitive assumptions on his character merely based on his looks. As I have told you, he is a disdainful, brooding sort of fellow, which must significantly lessen his chances of being considered handsome by anyone of sense with knowledge of his true character. I grant that I was surprised to hear he called on Uncle—and relieved he did not appear to exhibit his least favourable sides while there.

What Uncle says of him concurs with Papa's opinion. Formidable and forbidding, but respectable. Only one of these is a characteristic I would have hoped for in a husband. I suppose I should be glad—it is still one more good trait than was possessed by the previous man who planned on making me the companion of his future life. Of course, Mr Darcy's treatment of Mr Wickham proves that he is not always respectable. But at least he has the appearance of it. Papa seems convinced he will not be unkind to me—though perhaps it is only his own guilt he tries to assuage with such notions? I have told him not to feel guilty, for I do understand there was very little else that could be done.

As you have advised me, I am trying to reconcile myself with my fate. It is true that I should not put so much weight on what Mr Wickham has told me and, rather, try to focus on sketching my future husband's character on my own. But, Aunt, even if I discount the history I have learned from Mr Wickham, there is still very little of anything quite good to build on. I have not formed my opinion of him based on things learned from others—instead, these things only confirmed that which I had already discovered through my own observations.

Apart from the admittedly gallant effort of fishing me out of Mr Thompson's pond, he has done very little to recommend himself to me. Then, it is probable that I have not done much to recommend myself to him, either. After all, I am guilty of the ghastly crime of being born into a confined country neighbourhood. And of being utterly incapable of drawing or playing an instrument without flaw while elegantly dancing and singing in one modern language or another at the very same moment. By his calculations, I expect these are far heavier faults than any amount of arrogance, pride, and conceit put together. I suppose I should be happy—at least he finds me tolerable, and it must always be a happier alternative than being considered altogether intolerable!

Charlotte has been to call on me this morning. She is the only one of our friends and neighbours who does not look at me with either an air of disapproval, insufferable curiosity, or pity. Yet I can hardly bear her company, for Charlotte—ever practical—thinks I should rejoice in the excellent match the circumstances have brought forth. I am sure that she does not find Mr Darcy's company much more palatable than I do, yet one could almost think she envies me for my *good fortune*. Oh, that it could have been her taking a walk that day rather than your poor, sorry niece! I am sure that she would have made a more temperate and compliant mistress of Mr Darcy's estate than I ever could.

Mr Darcy has written to Papa to let us know that he will return from London in three days—with a new carriage, which pleases Mama exceedingly. Tuesday next is to be the wedding day. Punch and cake will be prepared for the servants, and an announcement for the *Times*, the *Courier* and the *Morning Post* has been drawn up. Mama and Jane have purchased most of the wedding clothes needed. In short, everything is or will very soon be ready for the event—that is, everything but my feelings on the matter.

After the wedding, we are to first travel to town and then, after Christmas, continue on to Derbyshire. My future husband's sister resides in London, which I presume to be the reason for our not travelling to Derbyshire directly. Needless to say, I should so very much like to see you, Uncle, and the children before you travel here, but I do not know if it will be possible. I expect that my time will not be my own. But let us hope that there will be time for at least a short visit. The mere thought of such a possibility cheers me immensely.

With all my love to you, Uncle, and the children.

Your affectionate niece,

E.B.

P.S. I know that, of late, I have been a selfish creature who can think of nothing but my own misery. I promise, I shall not always be so. I thank you for your patience—and I am sure Jane does as well, though she would never say it, as any time I spend writing to you about the gloomy turns of my life is time away from my complaining to her.

Longbourn, December 16, 1811

My dearest Aunt,

Now that it must all be too late, I believe I have discovered the source of the offensive fabrications so industriously circulated by the entire neighbourhood of late. It turns out that it was not Mr Darcy's rude behaviour we have to thank for our present circumstances; rather, it is all my own doing. By way of one small kindness to another, I have unwittingly brought upon myself an unkindness of quite unreasonable proportions.

You will perhaps remember that I told you earlier this year of the pretty frock I gave to our former maid Frances—and the subsequent proposal of marriage she received from Mr John Powlett, the Meryton tradesman. You might also remember Lettice Thompson, the daughter of our tenant Mr Thompson, and that she was not altogether pleased by the marriage and my supposed interference in the business. Well, Aunt, it seems that Mama might have had the right of it all along: I should never have made a gift of the old garment.

It was all revealed by Aunt Philips, who came to call on us earlier today. Apparently, she heard it from Miss Watson, who had heard it from her maid. When the news of my impending nuptials spread in Meryton, it seems Lettice Thompson insinuated to Miss Watson's maid that, if it were not for her, such an occurrence might never have taken place. By Aunt Philips's account, she refused to elaborate on her meaning—but it must all be clear. It was at Mr Thompson's pond, after all, where this string of misfortunes began. Who else would have seen us that day? Who else would bear such a grudge as to see fit to ruin my reputation for the sake of spite?

Stupid, hateful girl! What grief, what misery her small-minded vindictiveness has brought upon me! And upon our entire family.

Intolerable! It is fortunate that I am to quit Longbourn tomorrow; if I were to ever see her again, I cannot tell what I would do.

Jane, of course, thinks that it must all be some sort of a misunderstanding. Mr Thompson is a respectable farmer and, while we do not move in the same circles, we have known the family all our lives. As children, Jane and I sometimes played in the woods with Lettice and her sisters. She is not one year my junior. Jane cannot fathom that she could have intended to cause such harm. And perhaps it is so—perhaps she devised some spiteful gossip without thinking of the possible consequences. But I cannot forgive her for it. By the whole account of it, it does not appear as though she is looking for my forgiveness.

It is late at night and I am sitting in my room alone, writing by the light of a candle. My last night in this room—my last night home. Outside, the rain is falling slowly but steadily, which well fits my mood. My wedding clothes sit in a trunk by the door, along with the very few other things I shall take with me to my new, strange life. The frock I am to wear for the service tomorrow hangs in the closet—Sarah had hung it by the bed, but I confess that I moved the offending thing out of my sight. It is the same colour as the one I gave to Frances, which I suppose has some dubious poetry to it.

I do not expect sleep will find me, but I think I must try. You, Uncle, and the children have all my love, as always. I know that even though you are twenty-four miles away from here, all your thoughts will be with me in the morning.

By noon tomorrow, I shall no longer be Miss Elizabeth Bennet of Longbourn, Hertfordshire. When you next write to me, you must address your letter to Mrs Elizabeth Darcy, of Pemberley, Derbyshire. I believe it might take some time for me to get to know her. But I have no doubt that, in the end, I shall like her the best of all the Darcys.

Indeed, she might be my only friend.

Your loving niece,

E.B.

CHAPTER FOUR

---◁◆▷---

Mad, Bad and Dangerous to Know

The White Horse Inn, Leicester, December 30, 1811

My dearest Jane,

A thousand apologies for the gloomy epistle I sent you last. If, for some reason, you have not yet received it, I humbly beg of you to burn it without so much as a peek when you do. Of course, I know you have. While being in town felt to me much like being at the far end of the world, I am sure the Royal Mail does not share my sentiments.

It is a wretched beginning, indeed, that after less than a fortnight of married life, I should have already turned into one of those sharp-tongued old wives whose letters are filled with nothing but complaints and grievances. I shall try to mend my ways, I promise.

If for some reason I do not succeed, you will always have Aunt Gardiner to commiserate with—she has received more miserable missives from me of late than I dare to count.

In my defence, it must be said that, when I penned my last, I was quite convinced I had sunk into the darkest depths of despair. I have since come to my senses, much thanks to our dear sister Mary, who wrote to me not two days ago. She was kind enough to remind me that the only place I have sunk into recently is Mr Thompson's pond. How sweet of her, do you not agree?

As I am sure you can imagine, I was very grieved indeed to find out that Miss Bingley should have become so ill so soon after our departure. I suppose it was not entirely unexpected—she did look a bit wan when I last saw her at the wedding breakfast. I only hope her illness will not keep her brother in town too long; it seems untoward that they should have travelled thither in the first place, her being so *very gravely ill*. Do tell me again, what malady is it that ails her so?

I cannot express how happy I was to hear that our little cousin Thomas has started talking. I can only imagine how many tales he must have to tell, having looked at the world around him for two whole years without being able to tell a soul about all that he has seen. Tell me, are the Gardiners with you still or have they departed already? It saddened me to no end that I was not able to see them when in London—but, as both you and Aunt know rather too well, those first days were far too disquieting for me to even dare propose such a thing, and then it was too late. Even more, I wish that I was still there with you. I should so have liked to spend more time with you all, to spend one last Christmas at Longbourn.

Aunt has written a long letter to me, describing in great detail all her memories of the village of Lambton and its surroundings, no doubt trying to ease my mind and to give me something happy to look forward to. I daresay she has succeeded—Lambton sounds like a dear little place.

After two days of travelling, we are currently in Leicester. We are to leave here in the morning and should reach Pemberley before nightfall, if the weather allows. I do not know if I long to see the place or dread it. My husband sits across the room from me, reading a book—or at least graciously pretending to read, for I do not think he has turned the page once since he sat down. We have not exchanged too many words since that unfortunate quarrel on our first night as a married couple; it seems wiser to be quiet. It feels odd, still, to be in a room alone with him, a virtual stranger with whom I am to spend the rest of my life.

The days have grown steadily colder since we left Hertfordshire. The bricks and sheepskins kept us warm enough on our journey here, but I do believe that, if it gets much colder, we might see some snow before long. This morning, the air was so cold that I could see my own breath as we stood in front of the inn at Milton-Keynes waiting to board the carriage. It was supposed to be waiting for us, not the other way around, but there had been some mishap at the last moment. Needless to say, my husband was quite displeased. He did not say much, but his expression bore a great resemblance to a storm cloud. I have come to know that this is his way.

I shall end here; the maid has arrived to announce that supper will be served soon. I shall write to you again as soon as we reach Pemberley, though I am sure that anything I have to say will pale in comparison to Miss Bingley's meticulous descriptions of its many charms. Please let me hear from you again soon, and give my love, etc. to Mama, Papa, Mary, Kitty, Lydia, and everyone else who is inclined to receive it—but not to Lettice Thompson, mind you. If you see her on the street, I advise you to lift your chin as high as you can and walk right past her.

Affectionately yours,

E.B.

E.D.

Pemberley House, January 2, 1812

My dearest Jane,

I am sitting at the morning room window, gazing at a view that I suspect might make Lettice Thompson wish it had been her in the pond that day instead of myself. Outside, the wind is sweeping through the gardens, coming and going in furious gusts, making even the great Spanish chestnuts tremble and bend their backs like old, weary men. I long for warmer days when I can escape this house and sit writing under the chestnut trees instead of watching them from afar. I wonder if sitting under a tree with a book or paper and quill is considered fitting behaviour for the mistress of Pemberley?

There was no letter from you when we arrived the day before yesterday. I hope it is due to some delay in the post and not because you are afraid to write me after that ghastly missive I sent while in town. You should not worry for me. I am well. Or, if not quite well just yet, I am sure that I soon will be. We have argued again, but I expected nothing less when I married such a man. My husband might have had different expectations—but I believe that by now he is rather well acquainted with my ability to hold my own in an argument.

I have spent the morning today touring the house with the house-keeper, Mrs Reynolds. You can guess how much it pains me to ever admit Miss Bingley being right about anything or anyone, but I confess that I am glad she was right about my husband's library—like the chestnut trees, it is truly magnificent. It is as well that it should be so grand, if we are to spend all our evenings in the same manner as we have done thus far. Alas, it seems that my powers of deduction have yet again been bested by Miss Bingley for, when we stayed at Netherfield, she professed me to be a great reader who has no pleasure in anything else. I did not admit to it then, but it seems that she might have had the right of it, after all!

As you will remember from that letter we shall not mention again after this, my husband has declared himself less than pleased with the idea of us entertaining my relatives here at Pemberley. His relatives, however, seem to be another matter entirely. To my surprise, I did not get to meet Miss Darcy in London—there had been some last-minute changes to the arrangements (I can guess why), and she decided to spend Christmas in the country with her aunt and uncle. Now I have been told to expect her tomorrow afternoon along with a cousin of the Darcys—a colonel in His Majesty's army.

Mrs Reynolds mentioned in passing that my husband had invited the colonel's parents as well but that they were unable to come. I wonder if that, too, was on my account? After all, I have been told by *some* that marriage to me could be considered a degradation, and that there might be some family obstacles which could have prevented our marrying altogether in other circumstances. I must wonder why *some* think that a marriage would ever have even entered the discussion in other circumstances?

But I digress. As I said, I am to expect Miss Darcy and the illustrious colonel tomorrow, and I confess to feeling somewhat daunted. The house is so big that I can barely find my way from the front door to my chamber. What if I get lost? Would not that make a fine impression? Mrs Reynolds asked me if I had any preferences for the menu tomorrow and, as I did not have the vaguest idea what sort of dishes would be considered suitably grand by my husband, I simply asked Mrs Reynolds if she knew Miss Darcy's favourites. She seemed pleased with my answer so, at least on that account, I believe I shall be saved from any embarrassment.

I am half agony, half hope when it comes to the arrival of my new sister: agony, because I fear that our friend Mr Wickham was as right about her character as he was about my husband's; and hope, because I dearly hope that he was not! There are several portraits of her hanging in different rooms of the house (one is looking down at me from above a mantelpiece as we speak) and I have spent a good part of my tour this morning staring at them, trying to divine her character. The one in the portrait gallery made me shiver a little and, after seeing it, I felt confident that Mr Wickham had been right. However, the one in the music room made me think I should give her a big hug and a pat on the head for comfort. I wonder which painter has hit closer to the mark?

Do write to me, Jane dear, and tell me all the news from Long-bourn. I want to hear every significant thing—and every insignificant one, too. Has Mr Bingley returned yet? Is Mary still reading Fordyce, or have you caught her sneaking about with a copy of *Udolpho* hidden in the folds of her apron? Have Kitty and Lydia stopped bickering over my green frock? If not, tell them that I have changed my mind and shall take it with me on my next visit, whenever that may be. And if Papa is still bent on blaming himself for what has happened, do tell him to stop immediately and to write to me as soon as he can. I miss him dreadfully.

I have the strangest feeling that I am being spied upon. I shall close now and report back to you as soon as I have caught the culprit.

Yours ever,

E.D. (See? I am learning.)

Pemberley House, January 4, 1812

My dearest Jane,

I have received your letter (finally—there had been some confusion on the way, and it was quite misdirected), read it thrice over, and still I am not sure what to think of it. Are you sure Miss Bingley really means to say that none of their party will return to Hertford-shire this winter? Or could it rather be that she thinks they *should not* return? Truly, Jane, I never heard of a doctor who claimed country air to be bad for anyone's constitution! Even if Miss Bingley insists that it is so, what does it signify to her brother? Mr Bingley is not ill, is he? He seemed perfectly healthy and unharmed by the Hertfordshire air the last time I saw him.

As for Miss Bingley's allusions to any alliance anticipated between her brother and Miss Darcy, I do not believe a word of it. I have spent most of yesterday and the entire morning today in the company of said lady, and not once has she mentioned Mr Bingley. I mentioned him in passing yesterday, but she only nodded and smiled, more out of politeness, I think, than of any particular interest in hearing news of him. Oh Jane dearest, do not let Miss Bingley's venomous words poison your mind. I am sure that Mr Bingley will return any day now—and if he does not, perchance you might consider spending a few weeks with the Gardiners? I am sure little Thomas, Edward, and their sisters would love to spend more time with Cousin Jane. Of course, it would allow you and Aunt to double your efforts in cheering me, as you would not need to spend precious time writing to each other!

Miss Darcy and Colonel Fitzwilliam, along with Mrs Annesley— the lady with whom Miss Darcy has been living in London— arrived yesterday afternoon with much less commotion than I had expected. My husband was acting uncommonly impatient the whole morning, pacing back and forth from one window to another, looking at his pocket watch every half-minute. I could understand his uneasiness—the winds were still high, and it had started to snow the previous night. Had it been you in that carriage, I know I would have been wretched with worry until I saw you arrive safely to us. I almost felt like saying some words of comfort, but what is one to say in a situation like ours? It seems to me that every time we speak of anything other than the most mundane matters, an argument of some sort ensues.

The morning seemed to draw on forever but, in the end, our guests did arrive, not much late and mostly unaffected by the weather. I feel rather foolish now for ever having fretted over their reception of my person. Colonel Fitzwilliam is about thirty. He is not what I would call handsome but in person and address most truly the gentleman. If there are family members objecting to my marriage to Mr Darcy, he is certainly not one of them.

Miss Darcy's opinions on the matter are more difficult to decipher. She speaks very little and, when she thinks we are not looking, her wary gaze travels from myself to her brother and then back to me again. One thing I can tell for certain is that Mr Wickham has greatly misled us in his description of her character, so much so that I wonder if he did not do it for some clandestine purpose of his own? Miss Darcy is shy—painfully so. I imagine she would not dare to be proud, even should she wish it.

My husband's behaviour continues to perplex me. Dinner last night was a pleasant affair—not once since I left Hertfordshire have I been half so well entertained as I was last night. Unlike his cousin, the colonel proved himself to be a great conversationalist. We talked of the differences between Hertfordshire and Derbyshire, of travelling and staying at home, of new books and music. Even Miss Darcy seemed to enjoy the conversation, being so bold as to nod every now and then to agree with something her cousin said and, on occasion, even offering a smile or two.

Not my husband. He just sat at the end of the table in all his austerity, giving clipped answers whenever his cousin tried to include him in the conversation. Perhaps he is displeased with my crude country manners.

Oh Jane, I try to understand him, but I do not get on at all! I would have thought that he would be pleased to have some company besides myself. We have sat in silence for days on end, looking at the walls or pretending to read books, trying to avoid conversation. It must be as much of a strain to him as it is for me. And yet, instead of rejoicing at the first chance of easy, pleasant conversation, he chose to sulk all night. The colonel seemed to find his brooding silence amusing, but perhaps it is because he has known my husband so long and is, therefore, better used to being at the receiving end of his infuriating stares?

Remember when I told you in my last that I had an odd feeling I was being spied upon? Well, as soon as I had closed my letter to you, I started a thorough investigation on the matter. I did not catch the spy that day, but I found biscuit crumbs and two dead dragonflies (!) under the pianoforte in the music room—a telltale sign of mischief, do you not agree? With the arrival of our guests, I have not had the time yet, but I have every intention to catch the criminal mastermind as soon as I have a morning all to myself. I intend to leave a plate of biscuits under the pianoforte and wait to see who will appear to pilfer them. Our butler, Parker? Bonaparte's spies? Or perhaps my husband has a secret penchant for biscuits? Whoever it is, I plan to catch them and punish them mercilessly. After all, I have quite an infamous reputation already —I might as well live up to it.

Yours affectionately,

E.D.

P.S. Do give my love, etc. to everyone—despite being mad, bad, and dangerous to know, I am quite full of fond feelings when it comes to my family.

CHAPTER FIVE

The Dragonfly Spy

Pemberley House, January 7, 1812

My dearest Jane,

What a happy surprise awaited me this morning when I opened your letter and found myself in possession of not one, but three letters from home! I am so glad you were able to convince Papa to write a few lines, and I was quite impressed to see that Lydia, too, had taken the time to write to her poor, old, married sister. I must confess, however, that my delight in seeing her take up such a useful pastime was somewhat diminished after perusing the contents of her missive. Did you know the latest rumours have it that I was never actually *in* Mr Thompson's pond but rather waited in the woods for Mr Darcy to approach, and then—after seeing him come in my direction—wet my dress and pretended that I had fainted? Who knew I was such a devious creature? I certainly had no idea of it.

Apart from a small army of servants bustling about the house, I am all alone this afternoon. The ever-present winds seem to have abated for a day at least, and my husband and the colonel are gone to tour the estate. Miss Darcy and Mrs Annesley have gone to Lambton to visit the milliner's and some other shops. I was asked to join them but declined—I thought that after four days of straining to overcome her shyness and be sociable for my sake, my new sister deserved a little respite from my company. I would very much like to see Lambton, but I suppose I shall have time for that later. More time than I wish to think of.

I have finally set my trap for the Dragonfly Spy today. I have placed a plate of freshly baked gingerbread under the pianoforte and am now sitting in the room next to the music room, the door left slightly ajar so I can see if anyone comes in. It has been half an hour already and no one has yet appeared, but I am convinced that the scent of cinnamon wafting through the air will tempt the culprit to show himself eventually. He had best make his attempt soon, though, or there is a good chance that there will be nothing left once he arrives. The scent *really* is quite delightful.

Parker has just come to announce that a carriage is approaching the house. Who can it be? Is Parker cleverly trying to lure me away so that he can sneak into the next room and purloin the gingerbread? I suppose there is no helping it; I must go and greet the mysterious guests. I shall tell you later whether someone has actually arrived or if I have simply fallen victim to Parker's cunning ploy.

Still January 7—Dear Jane. Since writing the above, something most unexpected has happened. It is late at night, but I am too restless to sleep. If my eyesight is ruined due to writing in the fading light of the candle, we have Lady Catherine de Bourgh to thank for it.

I am sure you remember that our dearest cousin Mr Collins was quite upset at my union with Mr Darcy. Shortly before he stormed out of Longbourn in November, he declared to me that his esteemed patroness—and now, to the infinite delight of both myself and said lady, my aunt—Lady Catherine de Bourgh would be quite displeased with my marrying her nephew.

As I did not hear a word from her ladyship before the wedding despite our cousin's ominous threats, I did not spare the matter much thought. This afternoon, however, has taught me that making idle threats is not something we can count among our dear cousin's many faults. Lady Catherine is, indeed, most seriously displeased with my marriage—or as she prefers to call it, that patched-up business with her poor nephew—and has now taken the trouble of disrupting her visit with Lord and Lady Fitzgerald at Ashbourne to come here and personally inform me of her displeasure.

Oh Jane, I confess I am so vexed that even Mama would be proud of me. On the matter of our marriage being a patched-up business, I am inclined to agree with her ladyship. As for the rest of what she had to express, not so much. I shall not repeat all of the things she had to say of my person; suffice it to say that I have never been so thoroughly insulted. While quite adept at slandering me, I am sure even Lettice Thompson would find that there is still a great deal more she could learn from Lady Catherine de Bourgh.

According to my new aunt, not only have I ensnared my husband to marry me with my feminine arts and allurements (I was tempted to laugh at this—if the man did not find me handsome enough to tempt him in a ballroom, I daresay finding me soaking wet and covered in mud did little to improve his opinion!), I have also ruined forever the hopes of another young woman: Miss Anne de Bourgh. I had already learned from Mr Wickham that such a union had been planned, but now I am told it was nothing less than the very fondest wish of both Lady Catherine and my husband's mother that Mr Darcy marry Miss de Bourgh. I wonder if it was his fondest wish, as well. Perhaps that would explain his sour mood of late.

Alas, while he might have a *tendre* for his cousin, it seems that there is little love lost between my husband and his aunt. He and the colonel arrived from their tour of the estate just in time to hear some of the more memorable things she had to say to me—and I confess, I never imagined I could be as pleased to see my husband as I was at that moment.

To the utter dismay of Lady Catherine—and my unexpected delight—it turns out that the only person my husband allows to decry my connexions is himself. I know that he is as little pleased to be married to me as I am to be married to him, and he has made his thoughts of my family abundantly clear. Yet, to his aunt he showed nothing of it. Instead he declared that I was a gentleman's daughter and that, if he did not object to my connexions, they could be nothing to his aunt. It was truly quite impressive. As disagreeable as my husband can be, he does have his gentlemanlike moments.

At present, the recalcitrant aunt rests in one of the more distant guest rooms, to be sent back to Ashbourne in the morning. The colonel tells me that I have himself and my husband to thank that I did not receive a visit such as this before the wedding. It seems her ladyship had every intention to pay a call at Longbourn, but the gentlemen prevented her. Do tell Papa—I am sure he will be sorely disappointed to hear that he has so narrowly missed the chance of meeting our cousin's noble patroness.

I am at a loss as to why she has come now. If there were some way to undo all that has happened, I would do it—even at the risk of pleasing Lady Catherine. But I am married. There is nothing to be done for it. Like the rest of us, she will simply have to live with it.

With no winds sweeping through the valley tonight, the house is eerily quiet, and my candle has nearly burned out. Next door to me sleeps my husband—for better, for worse. After supper, I was summoned to his study to hear an unprecedented apology. He said he hoped I was not too badly wounded by the reprehensible conduct of his aunt. I told him that with such charming relatives of his own, it was no wonder he found mine so lacking in decorum. I now rather regret my impertinence.

I shall close now and see if sleep will find me.

Affectionately, your very obstinate and headstrong sister,

E.D.

P.S. It has just occurred to me that, unless the servants have found it and removed it, the plate of gingerbread is still under the pianoforte. I am sure Lady Catherine would disapprove.

Pemberley House, January 9, 1812

My dearest Jane,

Lady Catherine is gone back to Ashbourne, and Pemberley is quiet and calm again. As if somehow aware of her ladyship's departure, the sun has finally ventured out from the cover of clouds this morning, and the air is crisp and bright. Bundled in my warmest clothes, I made my way through the doors as soon as I had finished breaking my fast. In the gardens, some of the lanes had been swept clean by the gardeners. Everything else is covered in a pristine sheet of snow, so bright in the light of the winter sun that staring at it for too long a time could render one quite blind, I am sure.

I spent a good hour outside, walking between the snowy trees and flowerbeds until my toes were quite numb from the cold. Mrs Reynolds gave me what I imagine to be her sternest look when she saw me come in from the outdoors, and I obligingly attempted to look as penitent as I could—but truly, I could not feel very repentant. Perhaps I was out a bit longer than I should have been, but the clear air has helped me sort out my thoughts, and I feel better now than I have in days.

I can even feel thankful towards Lady Catherine. For all the unpleasantness that her visit brought upon us, I was glad to find out that, in the eyes of the world at least, my husband plans to stand by me.

I am happy that you are planning to take my advice and visit the Gardiners. The children will be delighted to have your company—and I am sure nothing could please our ill friend Miss Bingley better than seeing her dear Jane again. She did say that she longed for your company, did she not? And she must be feeling quite lonely, having been so very ill these many weeks. Indeed, it is most convenient. Despite the cold you suffered at Netherfield, the last two and twenty years have proved you quite resistant to any serious maladies caused by country air and, unlike her friends in London, you can therefore visit as often as you like without being in any danger of catching whatever ails her.

I am enclosing a small gift so you can see how, despite my manifold complaints, married life has improved my character. Relieved to see a certain lady depart the estate, Mrs Annesley, Miss Darcy, and I spent a quiet afternoon yesterday embroidering. You, of all people, know my tendency for haphazard stitches and unfinished work, but Mrs Annesley has proved herself to be quite the patient teacher. I advise you to pay particular attention to the little roses in the corners—I have mastered an entirely new pattern!

Mrs Annesley is a genteel, agreeable sort of woman with a great fondness for all things practical. She cannot be more than five and thirty, I believe, widowed at an early age, and has been with Miss Darcy since the past summer. She is rather too serious for my taste —when I told her the story of Mary, Kitty, and the Shrewsbury cakes, her only thought was of how awful it was that a whole pound of salt had been wasted in the attempt—but when I consider all her fine embroidery skills and gentle kindness towards Miss Darcy, I am willing to forgive her for it.

Miss Darcy, I think, is starting to warm to me. She has gone from answering my questions to occasionally posing a few of her own—and she had the courtesy to giggle when I told her and Mrs

Annesley that Aunt Philips did not visit for a month after Mama served her those cakes.

Oh Jane, I believe I shall make a dear friend of her yet—if her brother is of a mind to allow it, of course. Yesterday at dinner, I asked Miss Darcy if she thought we might have Shrewsbury cakes for dessert, and she nearly choked on her wine. The colonel laughed, but my husband looked most alarmed—perhaps he thinks I am a bad influence on his dear sister?

I shall close now and write again as soon as I have received your next. Perhaps by then I shall be addressing my letters to Gracechurch Street? In the meanwhile, give my love, etc. to everyone at home.

Yours ever,

E.D.

Pemberley House, January 15, 1812

My dearest Jane,

I hope this letter finds you well and comfortably settled in the blue room at Gracechurch Street. In my imagination, you are sitting by the window right now, looking out onto the bustling street or writing a long letter to me. So many happy memories are attached to that little room that I love it almost as well as my old chamber in Longbourn. Do you remember, many years ago, when we hid in the wardrobe that time Mr Campbell came to call upon you? To this day, I am sure Aunt knew we were in there but was kind enough not to inform Mama of it. I think it quite likely that I might have suffered apoplexy if I had had to listen to him recite another one of his pretty verses—and you, my dear sister, might now be married to the worst poet in all of England!

I am sorry to have alarmed you so with my account of Lady Catherine's visit—truly, there is nothing to worry about. She offended me with her words, but she has not injured my spirit. Miss de Bourgh may have been disappointed in her hopes, but it was not of my doing, and no amount of scorn from her mother will persuade me to believe otherwise.

On a happier note, I am proud to inform you that I have caught the Dragonfly Spy! His name is Samuel Reynolds, and he is a respectable gentleman of six and a half. In the end, catching him turned out to be the easiest of endeavours—when I found him, he was hanging from one of my husband's bookshelves, the ladder having slipped from under his feet, so there was very little he could do to escape my notice. Nevertheless, I wish that I had had a few biscuits or a slice of gingerbread with me when I found him for, by the time I rescued him from his perilous situation, the poor lad was quite distraught. I daresay he will not try to climb the bookshelves again in the near future.

He sat on my lap for a quarter of an hour at least before he calmed down enough to tell me who he was and what he was doing in the library. It was a good thing that I had one of my newly embroidered handkerchiefs with me—though I do find it quite unlikely that little Mr Reynolds cared very much at all for my new, sophisticated rose pattern. After he stopped crying, he confessed that he had been told in a very strict manner not to leave the servants' quarters. He asked if I was very angry with him and if I was planning on sending him back to Bath. I told him I had no such plans, which seemed to relieve him a great deal—apparently *That Tommy Graham* is someone he would rather not share a home with again.

Now, I have not a clue of who *That Tommy Graham* is, but what I do know is that his crimes are heavy indeed. When young Mr Reynolds resided in Bath, Mr Graham tried to steal his collection of dragonflies on several separate occasions! And that, I learned, is what brought Mr Reynolds to our library yesterday morning.

In the past week he had—quite reasonably, in my opinion—started to suspect that one of our stable-boys was up to Mr Graham's old tricks. To prevent any attempts at thievery, Mr Reynolds had first hidden his box of dragonflies in the larder, but the cook had found it there and, as you might guess, was not pleased at all. Next, he had decided on the orangery but, after a long, sleepless night spent worrying that the suspect stable-boy might follow his tracks in the snow, he finally decided that the best place to hide his treasure would be the *piano nobile*—after all, if he had been very strictly told not to enter there, then surely the same rules would apply to the stable-boy.

I must say, I am quite impressed at his thorough nature. Apparently he has been in almost every room of the first floor in the past few weeks! I am glad it was I who finally found him out and not my husband. I have a suspicion that he would not be too pleased to discover we have a little spy in the house.

As you might have guessed from his last name, Mr Reynolds is the grandson of our housekeeper, Mrs Reynolds. From what I understand, he lived in Bath with his mother and father until recently, but then his father unexpectedly disappeared some months ago, leaving behind what Mr Reynolds says his mother calls 'a great deal of debt and trouble.' I feel utterly ashamed of myself for ever thinking that life has treated me unfairly.

After our most insightful chat, I delivered the wayward lad back to the care of his grandmother. The poor woman went quite pale when she saw us and gave little Samuel a glare so stern that he started sobbing again. After sending the boy on his way, Mrs Reynolds apologised to me profusely, but I told her there was absolutely no reason to. Her grandson is nothing short of delightful and, while it is probably true that he should not be lurking about the first floor, I confess I am glad that he was and find myself hoping I shall meet him again soon.

Miss Darcy and the colonel have entered the room and seem determined to lure me into joining them in a game of charades. Miss Darcy is quite convinced that I, and I alone, can come up with the answer to the supposedly clever riddle her cousin has concocted. By the smug look on his face, I can tell that he does not share her conviction.

I shall close now and report to you of my success later. Please write soon and tell me all the news from London—is it really true that everyone of fashion is wearing long sleeves now in the evening? Aunt Gardiner says it most certainly is so but, knowing my preference for short sleeves, I suspect that she might be teasing me.

Affectionately yours,

E.D.

CHAPTER SIX

Amour Propre

Pemberley House, January 19, 1812

My dearest Jane,

I am an utter fool. If you ever repeat to anyone what I am about to write, I swear I shall deny ever writing such a thing and declare you a liar of the most scandalous nature. Of course, I trust your discretion above that of anyone else, so here it is, my terrible confession, entrusted to your care for you to laugh at and for no one else to ever hear of: if only I had listened to my mother.

Ever since I learned to walk, she has said time and time again that traipsing about the countryside is not a suitable form of exercise for a genteel lady. Every time I came home with a tear in my frock or my petticoats six inches in mud, she faithfully remembered to admonish me for my unseemly habits. But did I ever listen to her? Did I ever heed her advice? I most certainly did not—and now I must face the consequences.

One might think I would have learned my lesson that day at Mr Thompson's pond; certainly that was a fair example of the trouble a girl can get into whilst walking in the woods unaccompanied. Instead it seems I have learned absolutely nothing. Thus, I am doomed to be confined to my bedchamber for at least a fortnight—nursing a sprained ankle and a severely bruised *amour propre*.

The day before yesterday was another one of those charming crisp winter days, and I could not resist going for a walk even if it was somewhat windy and more than a little chilly. I was rambling by a little pond amidst the trees (yes, dear sister, you have read correctly—a pond) when suddenly a furious gust of wind caught onto my scarf and hurled it onto the ice. I stepped most carefully onto the edge of the slippery surface—and, as I have already told you of the state of my ankle, I am sure you can guess what happened next. I beg you not to tell Papa, or he might reconsider his estimation of my intellect!

After a good quarter of an hour spent crawling towards the house in the snow—having made several futile attempts to stand—I resolved to never, ever go walking alone again and resorted to crying for help. And of course, it was none other than my husband who heard my cries. I do not know what he was doing walking in the woods, but I can tell you that my embarrassment was acute. A lesser man—or a man with a healthier sense of irony—might have laughed when I mentioned the words 'slip' and 'pond' but, stoic creature that he is, my husband merely raised his brow. While I looked elsewhere, thoroughly mortified, he undid the laces of my boot and examined my ankle. Then, without another word, he took off his greatcoat, settled it on my shoulders, and lifted me off the ground.

It took us quite a while to reach the house and, try as I might, I could not think of a single word to say. The feel of the coat wrapped around me, the dark look on his face, and the steady, stubborn rhythm of his steps—every single thing reminded me of the unfortunate events at Mr Thompson's pond. I am quite sure that he was thinking of the exact same thing. From now on, I plan to keep at least a mile between myself and any nearby ponds, lest he start to suspect there is some truth to the malice Lettice Thompson has been spreading.

I must admit that there is something to admire in the cool, calm way he faces adversity. (In his mind, I am sure that a penniless country-savage of a wife with a tendency to slip into ponds is most certainly an adversity!) He did not fuss when he rescued me from drowning in Mr Thompson's pond. He did not fuss when Papa asked him to marry me. He did not fuss today when he found me, sitting in the snow, squealing like a little piglet. Instead, as I have seen him do before, he simply assessed the situation and did what he thought needed to be done. After almost one and twenty years of Mama fussing over every little thing, I confess that I find the change oddly refreshing.

We quarrel more often than not, but he rarely raises his voice. The only time I have seen him truly lose his temper was the night of our wedding. On nine days out of ten, his sombre mien serves only to make me irritable. But on the tenth day, on the day I find myself in some grave trouble or another, he has a rather admirable tendency to come to my rescue. (Do tell Aunt I said so—she will be exceedingly pleased to hear that I have taken heed of her recent advice and am not looking at my husband only to find fault in everything that he does. I do so like to make her proud of me!)

I have spent the last two days confined to my bed, and my only small comforts have been Miss Darcy's constant company, a few well-chosen books some kind soul deposited on my bedside table while I slept—and your delightful letter. Whenever I find myself feeling gloomy, I re-read the passage describing the miraculous recovery of Miss Bingley. How peculiar that she could have been so very ill one day as to not be able to receive visitors, only to be revived enough to tour the shops on Bond Street on the next!

Oh Jane ! Truly, I am sorry she has treated you so abominably. But

I am glad her brother was there to witness her deceit. I would not be surprised if she had never planned to tell him you were in town. Perhaps now he will make his way to Gracechurch Street to explain his lengthened absence from Hertfordshire?

Please give my love, etc. to Aunt, Uncle, and the children—and add in a big, wet kiss to little Thomas, if you can. I hope that, between playing endless rounds of spillikins with our cousins and receiving calls from a certain gentleman, you will find time to write long letters to your poor, injured sister.

Yours ever,

E.D.

Pemberley House, January 25, 1812

My dearest Jane,

Thank you for your letter, both prompt in arrival and delightful in content. Nothing short of a letter from you could have lifted my spirits today, the sixth day of my self-inflicted seclusion. Do be so kind as to remember me to everyone in Gracechurch Street—as well as any *indifferent acquaintances* who happen to stop by for dinner.

Oh Jane, do take care! You say you are not so weak as to be in any danger now, but I daresay you are in very great danger of making a certain indifferent acquaintance as much in love with you as ever! He might not have seen your dear face for over a month, but I am sure not a day has gone by that he has not thought of you. I would even be so bold as to guess that, by the time you read these words of mine, he has already told you as much himself.

I am sitting on my bed, buried in a mountain of pillows, a bed tray on my lap so unsteady that it well deserved the alarmed look of the maid who came in to see if I needed anything, taking note of the ink bottle balanced precariously close to the pristine white sheets.

If the maid is prone to gossiping, I am sure the laundress is plotting ways to take my life even as I write. However, I am determined to receive as many letters as I can to break the monotony of my days, and surely the best way to attract new missives from other people is to send as many of my own as I can—even at the cost of a few ink-stained sheets.

My efforts are bearing fruit already for, in addition to Aunt Gardiner (whose description of Mr Bingley's behaviour at dinner, I must say, did not mention the word 'indifferent' once—I wonder why?), I received a very merry letter from Mary, Kitty, and Lydia yesterday. Mary, apparently, is as fond of her copy of *Sermons to Young Women* as she ever was—yet another thing we can blame upon our dear, pious cousin—and, after hearing of my latest misfortunes, immediately decided that I could benefit from a few well-chosen quotes on modesty and decorum. Lydia found the unsent missive on the side table in the sitting room and decided to add a few lines of her own that had, needless to say, less to do with decorum and more to do with certain members of the militia. Naturally, Kitty then demanded that she be allowed to add a few words, too—thus, I can now proudly declare myself an expert not only on Mr Fordyce's thoughts regarding feminine manners and Mr Denny's dispute with the butcher but also on the great variety of new ribbons available at Mr White's.

Mary had effectively crossed out some lines in the part Lydia had written—adding a note at the end to explain that they were simply not fit to be seen by anyone—and now I suppose I shall never find out what exactly it was that Mr Denny said to the butcher to upset him so—but I was much amused by the contents of the letter, all the same. I fear, however, that I should have kept my amusement to myself. I read the whole epistle aloud to Miss Darcy and Mrs Annesley last night, and something in it seemed to upset my new sister a great deal. As I find it unlikely there was anything to distress her in Mary's sage advice or Kitty's rambling tale of ribbons, I can only presume it was Lydia's mention of our friend Mr Wickham that caused her to plead a headache and quit the room quite unexpectedly.

I suspected it before, but now I am convinced there is more to Mr Wickham's connexion to the Darcys than he led me to believe. His account of Miss Darcy's manners I have already found quite false, but why should she flinch so at the mention of his name? Is it something he has done? Or has my husband simply poisoned his sister's mind against their father's favourite out of spite and jealousy? Somehow I cannot quite see him doing that—he is many things, but deceitful does not seem to be one of them. To be sure, he said as much himself on one memorable occasion.

Apropos my husband, he has been acting even more strangely lately than is his usual wont. Since the arrival of Miss Darcy and the colonel, we have been alone together only on a few, rare occasions—a good thing, I had thought, as we endured more uncomfortable silences and strained conversations in those first weeks together than I would have wished to endure in a lifetime. But now it seems he is determined to have more of them, and I am at a loss to understand why.

Every day since my accident, he has appeared in my room at one time or another, always managing to choose a moment when no one else is present, always fixed on the same strange routine. He asks me a few awkward questions regarding the state of my ankle, never seeming to pay much attention to my answers. He sits down on a chair by the bed, smooths his breeches, then jumps up again. He paces back and forth in an agitated manner or stares out of a window, making it clear that he is as uncomfortable as can be. Yet he always appears, day after day, without fail. It is all very odd.

Yesterday morning, after a considerable show of pacing and sighing, he sat back down again, and I almost thought that I was going to find out what he was about. But then Miss Darcy entered the room, and he jumped up again and left the room in great haste. Obviously, he has something on his mind, but what can it be?

Oh, dear, look at those blots! It seems that crossing is not the best of ideas when one is writing on a tottering bed tray. Perhaps I should add a second sheet—I am sure Mama would applaud me for the excess. So many mysteries abound in this house that one sheet is simply not enough to cover them.

However reluctantly, I shall close now and tell you more about the strange happenings at Pemberley in my next missive. Perhaps by then I shall have found out why my husband is determined to torture himself by spending so much time in my barely tolerable company, and what it is Mr Wickham has neglected to tell us!

Please accept my sincere wishes for many more dinners spent in quite common, indifferent company and give my love to Aunt, Uncle, and the children. What I would not give to be there with you!

Yours in affection,

E.D.

Pemberley House, January 27, 1812

My dearest Jane,

I hope you do not think it very bad form of me to start a new letter before I have received a reply to my last—I am quite simply too impatient to wait. I solemnly promise to wait for your next before I post this one. As I write, I am sitting by the bow window in the music room, looking out into the darkening night, listening to Miss Darcy play the pianoforte. (She plays uncommonly well, I think—particularly so if one manages to catch her when she thinks no one is listening.) Even though a fire is blazing not too far from me, I can feel the cold settling in, seeping in through the windows. The sun has been mocking me these past many days, sending tempting rays through my window to remind me of all I am missing because of my foolish accident. But somehow, I feel sure that it will snow again tonight.

The reason I am so eager to write to you again is three-fold. I am sure that Aunt is peeking over your shoulder while you read, demanding to know how I have reached the music room with my hopelessly invalid ankle still very much in pain, so I shall do you both a kindness and save that part for the last! As Mr Fordyce reminds us, it is by patience that a lady must triumph, and what better way is there to learn patience than to try it a little every now and then?

My first and foremost reason for taking up my pen is to offer you an apology—one that is as belated as it is heartfelt. It seems that married life has made me in equal measures blind and selfish for, up until this morning, I had not realised the full enormity of the trouble I put you through with my correspondence. I had expected Mama would express some disdain over not being allowed to read my letters to you but, as you have not so much as hinted at any trouble, I did not spare the matter much thought. I should have known better.

I received a letter from Mama this morning and, judging from its contents, she has been truly merciless in her attempts to pester you for my missives. Oh, dear sister, I am so very sorry! You truly are the kindest, most unselfish person I know. And the most steadfast! I am sure that even the Spanish Armada would not get past you if you set your mind to it—all the same, I am glad you are in London now, far from the prying eyes at Longbourn.

To console Mama over having such secretive, ungrateful daughters, I have written her a long letter this morning, describing every little detail of the house I thought might interest her, sealing it carefully after I was finished and marking it *Private* to complete the effect. I expressly told her not to tell anyone how incandescently happy I am living in a great big house with a wealthy husband and an army of servants to take care of my every need. I am sure that nothing will please her better than to be able to share these confidences with the neighbourhood in general, and that vile Thompson girl (her words, but I find myself agreeing with her for once) in particular. It is my hope that more regular letters addressed directly to her will dissuade her from her desire to read those addressed to you.

In addition to Mama's sulky epistle, I also had the honour of receiving a remarkably short and mysterious missive this morning hidden in a letter addressed to Miss Darcy.

Dear Mrs Darcy,

Do allow me to express my most sincere congratulations on your recent nuptials.

Most sincerely, Miss de Bourgh

And that was all! Rather irregular, do you not agree? What is one to think of such a letter? I would like to believe she is genuinely pleased —perhaps she had no more desire to marry my husband than I did and is now glad to be spared of the obligation—but I am suspicious of her assertions of sincerity. In my experience, people who declare themselves to be *most* sincere are rarely very sincere at all, and Miss de Bourgh has done so twice! Do tell me what you think and please ask that Aunt do so as well. Should I send her a reply? If so, shall I write sincerely or *most* sincerely? I would ask Miss Darcy, but I do not wish to chance offending her twice in the space of a single week.

Lastly, I wish to tell you something that I hope will please you, for I know how you have worried for my sake these past months. Colonel Fitzwilliam is to leave Pemberley on the morrow and, whilst his last day here has been tinged with a measure of wistfulness, it has also been the happiest I have spent since my arrival. Yesterday, as my husband arrived to do his self-imposed daily duty of gloomily stomping around my chamber for a quarter of an hour, I asked him if we might not do something special today to give the colonel a proper farewell.

He seemed reluctant, to say the least, and I was quite offended when he told me that I would do best to put such nonsense out of my head and stay in bed until my ankle was fully healed—but then, this morning, he showed up again quite unexpectedly and offered an apology. I much suspect that his sister put him up to it but, frankly, I do not care what brought on his sudden change of mind. He has been on his best behaviour the whole day; I imagine this is what Mr Wickham meant when he said that my husband has the ability to please when he so chooses.

We spent the afternoon in the library, where the colonel entertained us with stories of his life in the army (though I do suspect he left out some of the more unpleasant details for the benefit of myself and Miss Darcy), and my husband read aloud to us at his sister's behest. After dinner (boiled fowl, the colonel's favourite), we moved to the music room where, to Miss Darcy's horror, the colonel had a footman bring in a bowl of brandy and raisins for a game of snap-dragon. My husband looked exceedingly uncomfortable but, after some cajoling from his cousin, deigned to pluck a raisin from the flaming bowl.

Right then, sitting in the darkened room, looking at that austere man bent over the bowl in an awkward angle, trying to look dignified while snatching a raisin from amidst the flaming liquid, his cousin and his sister laughing at him freely, I felt it. It was only a fleeting moment, gone as soon as it had appeared but, for a moment, I felt like—home.

I do not expect to befriend my husband; we view the world too differently for that. But if we could learn to put our differences aside when we are together, as we have today, then perhaps...

I am very fond of Miss Darcy, and I grow more fond of her each day I spend with her. The house is charming, the servants kind and efficient. Meeting the colonel has taught me to hope that not everyone connected to my husband will shun me. Now, if only I could learn to tolerate my husband and he could tolerate me, then perhaps there would be some hope of a happier future yet.

I have changed my mind—I truly am too impatient to wait. I plan to seal the letter now for the morning post. I shall write to you again when I receive a reply to my last. Kiss the children for me and give my love, etc. to Aunt and Uncle.

Affectionately yours,

E.D.

P.S. If you are still wondering how I got into the music room—and into the library, for that matter—I shall reward your patience with my ramblings and tell you directly: my husband once again deigned to defy propriety and carried me. I suspect Miss Darcy might have mentioned my plans of procuring a walking stick and hobbling down the stairs myself.

CHAPTER SEVEN

That Dear Boy

Pemberley House, January 29, 1812

My dearest Jane,

I am sitting in my private sitting room (for what else is one to do in a sitting room? Standing, I am sure, would be an offence to the sensibilities of such a refined space—how fortunate that I am as of yet unable to do so for any great length of time), warmly dressed, and my feet firmly tucked under a blanket—yet I feel chilled to the bone. Outside, the winds are blowing again, tempestuous and wild and so heavy with snow that, when I look out the nearby window, I can barely see the bridge that crosses the stream in front of Pemberley even though this room is almost directly above that spot. I received your letter earlier this morning and, while I was delighted to have it, I could not help but feel sorry for the poor man who carried it here through the storm raging outside. To console my conscience, I have decided that he was not sent back outside after he delivered the post but, rather, sits by a roaring fire in the kitchens even now, a cup of hot soup in his hands, chatting merrily with one of the footmen. I dearly hope that I am right.

I am afraid I must start my missive by disabusing you and Aunt of any fanciful notions regarding my husband having a secret *tendre* for me and ask you to prepare for something dreadful instead. He is not in love with me, despite what you both have so readily assumed. With utmost certainty—not. To him, I am not merely the country-savage of a wife with questionable relations and a propensity to end up in perilous situations. Indeed not. To these already established faults, I must now also add something more substantial: that is, my being an unforgivable flirt and a fool of the first order.

After reading these bitter words, would you be very surprised if I told you that my husband and I have engaged in yet another quarrel? Although I do think that to call it a quarrel does not quite do justice to the livid nature of the dispute—I believe we might have even outdone the infamy that was our wedding night. I am vexed; I am grieved; I am every possible kind of upset. My astonishment at what has passed increases with every review of it. How foolish I now feel that, but two days ago, I thought there might be some hope for the future still.

The colonel left us early in the morning yesterday. Having said my goodbyes before I retired the night before, I did not wish to bother my husband by having him assist me down the stairs to see his cousin off. I did not wish to bother him later in the day, either—very well, I admit, I did not wish to bother myself. Having him carry me has always been an awkward experience, to say the least, and the night before was the most awkward of all these occasions. I thought it perhaps best that I stay in my rooms until I am able to walk unassisted and thus asked to have dinner brought up to my room instead of going down to the dining room. A few hours later, I learned I had made a grievous mistake.

I was getting ready to retire when my husband appeared in my room, unannounced, ordering the maid to leave us with a rudeness I had never before seen him display to the servants. He poked the fire, drew the curtains, all with such force that I knew not what to think of it. Then he sat down on the chair that he often occupies, looked straight at me—and I realised that he was slightly in his cups.

Without preamble, he asked if I was very disappointed to see his cousin go. Foolishly, I mistook the reason for his harsh manner, imagining that he thought me rude for not having seen the colonel off that morning. I told him I was indeed very sorry to lose the colonel's company and that I hoped he might be able to visit us again soon.

He next asked me if the colonel's departure was the sort of loss that might be diminished by inviting another house guest—he suggested that I might like to invite you to Pemberley. After all the things he said about our family on our wedding night, you can imagine my surprise at such a suggestion! But I was delighted, too, for I thought that perhaps it meant he had started to reconsider his previous words. So I thanked him for his consideration but told him that you were presently in town and that I did not wish to interrupt your stay there—and of what happened then, the less said the better.

Oh Jane! I do not know how to tell you this, or even if I should, but at the same time I feel I must. It seems that, for the lengthy absence of Mr Bingley, we have my husband to thank as much as our dear friend Miss Bingley. I do not wish to pain you and would not tell you of this at all if I did not think that it might help you find happiness. It was not indifference that drove your suitor away but a misguided confidence in the counsel of an old friend.

While the invention of a ridiculous illness was surely all Miss Bingley's doing, it was my husband who first advised Mr Bingley to leave Hertfordshire based on a rather dubious account of observing your manner and seeing no symptom of peculiar regard towards his friend. My husband made the rather high-handed assumption that it was Mama, more than yourself, who had hopes for a future involving Mr Bingley and told his friend that he had best distance himself from our family.

Oh Jane! Mr Bingley loved you, and I am sure that he does still. If it were not for my husband's interference, he would never have left Hertfordshire.

I wish I could tell you this was the extent of our unfortunate argument and that, after I expressed my ire over my husband's officious behaviour, he had shown some contrition over his high-handed manner in return. Sadly, it was not to be.

Instead, to my great surprise, I learned that I have been quite shamelessly flirting with Colonel Fitzwilliam these past weeks, which served as some further proof of a supposed family weakness. Who would have thought? It seems that, not only have I unwittingly disgraced my husband and made a fool of myself in front of the servants, I have also set an appalling example for poor Miss Darcy. All this time, I thought I was just showing politeness and kindness to a person who is clearly very important to both my husband and his sister—how fortunate I am to have such a wise, perceptive husband to educate me on these matters.

After he had thoroughly aired his grievances over my conduct, I confess that any restraint I had was quite forgotten, and I could not resist returning the compliment. I told him it was my understanding that, of the two of us, he must be the one to possess the greater ability to act disgracefully towards those closest to him. Whatever one thinks of Mr Wickham, did my husband not, after all, ruin his prospects out of spite and jealousy?

I did not get to broach the topic with any great eloquence, for I was soon told that I was never to speak again of Mr Wickham in this house. The reason? I was given none. On this matter as in all others, I am to trust the superior wisdom of my husband, as a good wife ought. I am starting to suspect that Mary has been kind enough to send quotations from Mr Fordyce to my husband as well as to myself.

I do not know if I should be crying or laughing over the absurdity of it all. I am half hoping that my ankle might never heal so that I may remain hidden away in my rooms for the rest of my days. Unfortunately, the uncooperative thing is already showing significant signs of improvement. How am I ever to face my husband again after all that has been said and done? How can I spend the rest of my life tied to a man who thinks so poorly of me that he accuses me of flirting with a man who might as well be his brother? It is in every way insufferable!

Oh Jane, my dear, dear sister. Pray forgive me for once again laying my troubles at your door—or at least do not punish me so far as to exclude me from Netherfield; in regards to inviting my husband, you may do as you please.

Affectionately yours, etc.,

E.D.

Pemberley House, January 31, 1812

My dearest Jane,

Where should I begin? I believe I owe an apology—but to whom, I cannot decide. To you, certainly, for the bitter and hasty words of my last letter. I have come to learn that I would be wise to think first and write later. To Charlotte Lucas, quite likely, for not listening with more attention to her wise words about showing affection and encouraging love. To Miss Darcy, unequivocally, for distressing her with mentions of a man who has done her a grievous wrong. To my husband? I hardly know.

Yesterday morning, I awoke facing a dilemma. I had already

hidden one day in my chamber, and I would dearly have loved to bury further under the blankets, remain in bed all day, and pretend that the world outside my door did not exist. The more I thought of what had happened, the more furious I felt—at what my husband had done to you, at what he had accused me of. Furious, because the hesitant truce I thought we were heading towards had been so abruptly interrupted. I wished to avoid him at all cost but, at the same time, I felt it imperative that I did not.

I could not very well call for him to assist me, and I felt fairly confident that even if I might somehow hobble down the stairs myself, my physician would disapprove of such attempts most heartily. The stairs, I have been told, are absolutely out of the question until my foot has healed fully. In a fit of pique, I decided that my best option was to have two footmen carry me down in a chair.

Oh Jane, I have never felt so ridiculous in my life! By the time my questionable convoy reached the door of the family dining room, I was quite prepared to ask the footmen to turn around from sheer embarrassment. In the end, it turned out that I might as well have done that—for when I made my grand entrance to the dining room, attempting to look as icy and regal as one can manage in a wobbling chair, it turned out that my husband was not there at all!

Instead, I broke my fast with Mrs Annesley and Miss Darcy, who was equal parts distress and misery: misery, because she had chanced to hear parts of the infamous argument; and distress, though I did not know it then, because of something her brother had asked her to share with me.

Seeing Miss Darcy was the first thing that started to abate my anger. The poor girl was so upset over my disagreement with her brother, I could not help but feel sorrier for her than I did for myself. No matter what I think of my husband, in the eyes of Miss Darcy he is the finest man who ever lived. I much suspect that she has never raised her voice in his company—and I find it rather likely he has never done so either. To hear the bitter words exchanged in the midst of our argument must have felt to her like the worst sort of abomination.

The second thing to cool my temper—a letter. From my husband, entrusted in the care of Miss Darcy to give to me at the first opportunity in the course of the morning. Oh Jane, I do not know what to make of it all! When I first read the letter, I was so prepared to think ill of him, so persuaded he could have no explanation to give, I scarcely allowed for the possibility that there might be some justice to what he wrote. Now that I have read the missive many times over, I find I am no longer so sure of myself.

In the way he has acted towards you and his friend, I still find injustice. He might not have been able to ascertain your true feelings towards his friend, but I cannot see that he had the right to so presumptuously decide the lives of others. Then again, when one remembers the lack of propriety shown by the members of our own family on so many occasions, one cannot deny the credit to some of his assertions. The mere thought depresses me beyond anything I have ever known before—perhaps it is not my husband, after all, that we have to thank for driving away Mr Bingley, but our own family.

Of Mr Wickham's dealings with the Darcys, I now know more than I ever bargained for. At the behest of her brother, Miss Darcy came to see me yesterday afternoon and gave a detailed account of Mr Wickham's actions, though I could see how it pained her to speak of the matter. I do not wish to write the particulars in a letter; suffice it to say that my husband and his sister have been used extremely ill by said gentleman (I hesitate to even call him that).

I am wretched to think of how blindly I accepted all his falsehoods as the truth after so short an acquaintance. Mr Wickham might not be evil, but his deceitful nature and utter disinterest towards the well-being and happiness of anyone other than himself quite nearly make him so. I have written to Papa this morning and encouraged him to be more prudent about our family's future dealings with the officers.

Of my supposedly infamous flirtation with the colonel, the letter said nothing. After addressing the offences I had laid to his charge (this took him two whole sheets written in a very close hand!), my husband merely ended with a curt apology for his brutish behaviour and a promise that I should not fear such an occurrence taking place again.

To say I am vexed does not cover the multitude of thoughts that occupy my mind. On the subject of Mr Wickham, there can be no two opinions. I can think of neither him nor my husband and my new sister without feeling that I have been blind, partial, prejudiced, and absurd. Of the rest, I cannot fix my opinion. I feel quite reasonable and forgiving one minute, only to feel perfectly irate in the next. Worst of all, I cannot demand to discuss the matter through with my husband, as he has gone to Chesterfield, not to return for several days. On business, says the letter, but I am inclined to think that business has nothing to do with it.

Oh, dear! It seems that my letters grow more rambling and disconcerting by the day. I started this missive to apologise for the previous one, and now I find that this one became just as depressing as the last. Perhaps I should refrain from writing until I have happier news to share.

The next time I write to you, I promise it will be only to tell you of the oddly flavoured draught the cook concocted for Mrs Reynolds, who has been coughing quite badly for a week at least, or of the spectacularly boring book on horticulture I am trying to read at the recommendation of Mrs Annesley.

Until then, I am very affectionately yours, etc.,

E.D.

P.S. I almost forgot. A most peculiar thing happened this morning. I found a small parcel on my dressing table with a neatly folded note placed on top of it. *I have taken the liberty to deliver you a gift from an admirer*, the note said, *to prove that I am not always a jealous brute.* Inside the parcel—a dead dragonfly!

Pemberley House, February 4, 1812

My dearest Jane,

Where would I be without you? I have sent you one miserable missive after another, yet you always reply with such cheer and warmth. Whether it was your description of little Edward challenging Mr Bingley to a snowball fight or the fact that he actually accepted the challenge, I cannot tell—but your letter has made me laugh out loud for the first time in days, and for that I thank you heartily. In the midst of all the confusion of late, it feels good to know that there is at least one place in the world where happiness always abounds.

I can hardly imagine Gracechurch Street with enough snow to allow for snowball fights and snowmen at this time of year but, as you and Aunt have assured me that it is so, I suppose I must believe it. Both Mary and Charlotte tell me that Meryton, too, has been snowed in more than once this past month—a circumstance that seemed of little concern to either of them—but I understand that Lydia, Kitty, and Maria Lucas have been quite inconsolable over the matter.

Here at Pemberley, the winds have abated. A heavy layer of snow has covered everything and rendered the house and its surroundings eerily quiet. My elusive husband remains in Chesterfield, and Miss Darcy, Mrs Annesley, and I have gotten into a habit of spending our evenings huddled in the large armchairs by the fireplace in my sitting room, reading and embroidering. The state of my troublesome ankle is considerably improved and I can now move around without any great inconvenience but, as the sitting room is small and cosy, we have seen no need to move to the larger rooms down the stairs.

Poor Mrs Reynolds's cough has taken a turn for the worse, and she has been bedridden these past few days. I much suspect that the dubious draught the cook gave her had something to do with it— the apothecary has issued strict orders not to touch it again!

Ensuring that she stays in bed is proving almost as arduous a task as trying to run the household in her absence. I confess I have not taken enough time to familiarise myself with the daily affairs of the house; although I know that it is my home now, I have felt more like a guest than a mistress here. Now, elbow deep in solving quarrels between chambermaids and parlourmaids, and trying to assure the cook that there is no need to set up elaborate meals when it is only us three ladies occupying the house, I have come to realise how deeply indebted I am to Mrs Reynolds. Until now, the most I have done is to answer questions regarding my preferences on this matter and that, never understanding the amount of work that goes into running a household of such magnitude.

This morning, Parker informed me for the second time that he had caught Mrs Reynolds up and about despite the apothecary's orders. (Parker has a remarkable skill of looking utterly discreet while delivering every sort of gossip. His prowess in such matters would make half the ladies in Meryton green with envy!) Determined to put an end to such endeavours, I made my first unassisted trip down the stairs since my accident to see her myself. I never got to give the stern sermon I had planned upon, for I was distracted by not one but two remarkable stories involving my husband.

The first was related by little Samuel Reynolds, whom I found loitering outside his grandmother's door looking as grave as a boy of six-and-a-half possibly can. I sat down to chat with him and, in as good an imitation of Mama as I could manage, told him that people do not die of trifling colds. He was considerably cheered by the thought and, in return, told me a most interesting tale regarding the gift of a dragonfly I recently had the honour to receive.

He explained that my husband had come to his rescue in the stables one day, and just in the nick of time too, for the same cunning stable-boy that Mr Reynolds previously suspected of treacherous intentions had been trying to dare him into entering the stall of a particularly ill-tempered mare. Not only had my husband scolded the stable-boy quite thoroughly—which I can imagine without any great trouble—but he also let little Mr Reynolds sit atop his mount for a while with the very noble purpose of making said stable-boy envious. In return for this great kindness, little Mr Reynolds had offered to gift him with one of his precious dragonflies—an offer he had, apparently, quite solemnly accepted.

The second tale was shared by Mrs Reynolds quite by accident when I entered her room and told her of my amusing encounter with her grandson. Oh, that dear boy, she sighed and, while I assumed that she was talking about little Mr Reynolds, I soon discovered I was much mistaken. Shaking her head, she continued that if that dear boy had not offered to take Samuel and his mother in when her scoundrel of a son ran away, she did not know what would have become of them. Oh Jane! You can imagine my surprise when I realised 'that dear boy' was none other than my husband!

It seems that every day he stays away, I hear some new account of him to puzzle me further. Miss Darcy, who seems to have gained new confidence from the repeated assurances of both myself and Mrs Annesley that she is not to blame for what happened with Mr Wickham, has started a charmingly transparent campaign of praising her brother to me at every turn. I must admit I am amused by her efforts but, at the same time, I worry that she will be gravely disappointed when she realises her brother and I shall never become the happy couple she would wish us to be.

Yesterday evening, I managed to befuddle her by calling her a bluestocking when I noticed that she was perusing the letters of Mrs Chapone, her brow knitted in great concentration. I maintained that it was a compliment to her intellect, but she seemed quite shocked by the idea. However, she soon gathered her wits and retaliated by asking whether the volume in my hands was one of the books her brother had selected to be delivered to my room after my accident by the pond. I confess that my blush was much deeper than hers and that I could think of nothing very clever to reply.

I am quickly running out of space and must close now. Please remember me to everyone, and write to me as soon as you can manage.

Yours in sincere confusion,

E.D.

CHAPTER EIGHT

Ode to Hedgehogs

Pemberley House, February 6, 1812

My dearest Jane,

My husband has returned. I am sitting in my room, unable to sleep despite the lateness of the hour, and I can hear movement behind the door that adjoins my rooms to his. I wonder if it is very selfish of me to draw some strange form of comfort from the fact that it appears he, too, feels too unsettled to rest.

He had sent a note ahead telling us to expect him early on the morrow, but then he appeared unexpectedly, shortly after dinner, quite disheveled and in a most peculiar mood. Such was my surprise at his sudden appearance in the sitting room that I pricked my finger with the embroidery needle and let out a decidedly unla-dylike (and embarrassing) yelp.

Miss Darcy was all excitement to see him again, pummelling him with questions regarding his stay in Chesterfield. He answered her queries with his usual grave, laconic eloquence and seemed distracted to the point of giving offence. Miss Darcy did not seem to mind, however, looking as pleased as Punch every time he offered another monosyllabic grunt by way of an answer.

I suppose I should have guessed that she, too, was distracted with other plans, for he had not been in the room five minutes when she suddenly started to complain about a headache so severe that, not only did she have to excuse herself, she also took Mrs Annesley with her. I assure you that I have never seen a person suffering from an aching head smile so much. For all her reputed shyness, my new sister is turning out to be quite a sly creature.

Alone with my husband for the first time since our argument, I suddenly found it very difficult to devise anything sensible to say at all. To fill in the uncomfortable silence that settled in the room after Miss Darcy and Mrs Annesley had gone, I asked him if he had had a pleasant trip—not at all—and if the roads had been snowy—yes, very. He moved to sit in the armchair closest to mine and, while I cannot say quite what it was or if it was perhaps just my nerves playing tricks on me, something in his tense, awkward manner suddenly reminded me of the way he looked on the night of our wedding just before he tried to bestow that unfortunate kiss on me. I suppose I should be glad that Parker chose that particular moment to see if my husband required supper after his long journey.

Oh Jane! I never knew I was such a cowardly thing but, as soon as Parker appeared, I sprang up from my chair and bid my husband a good night, rushing out of the room as if my very life depended on it. During his absence, I had imagined the conversation we would have on his return a thousand times over. At times, I thought it would be a sensible, rational discussion on our situation; at others, I let my ire take over my reason. Never once did I imagine myself as I was this night, tongue-tied and confused, unable to put two words of sense together.

I have always prided myself on my quick wit and easy conversation, but it seems now that I have lost a good deal of it somewhere on the way from Longbourn to Derbyshire. Conversing with my husband has always been a strenuous task, but now the mere thought of it seems next to impossible. I wish to reprimand him for the unfeeling things he has said about my family and friends, but then I remember his kindness to little Samuel and his mother. I wish to thank him for the thoughtful gift of books when I was ill, but then I remember his hurtful words regarding my behaviour towards the colonel. I do not know what to say to him. Are we to talk of the weather and the condition of the roads for the rest of our lives?

It is close to midnight, and the noises behind the adjoining door have quieted down. I suppose I should try to sleep—perhaps the morning will find me my rational, cheerful self again. To think that, only a few months ago, I was walking down the path towards Mr Thompson's pond, blissfully unaware that my blithe, careless step that morning would lead me to this moment. How long ago that day now seems.

Give my love, etc. to everyone in Gracechurch Street.

Yours in affection,

E.D.

Pemberley House, February 11, 1812

My dearest Jane,

Et tu, Brute? I am sure you can guess how remarkable I found it that you managed to dedicate an entire half a sheet to describe the particular words my husband had chosen to use in his letter to Mr Bingley! I daresay that he would be quite shocked to learn that the gentleman in question chose to show it to you—and thoroughly displeased to discover that you then shared its content with me! As I have little doubt that this clever little plot to make me think better of my husband has been heavily influenced by our dear aunt, I shall not blame you overmuch.

I hope that you will be quite proud of me when I say that you and Aunt can give up your newly found scheming ways, for my husband and I have made great progress in these past few days. After two uncomfortable dinners spent discussing in exhausting detail the differences between the murals in the gallery and the murals in the family dining room, I decided that to spend many more evenings this way would simply be insupportable (and unhealthy, I might add, for Mrs Annesley was already complaining of the strain the endless inspection of the ceilings was causing to her neck). Thus, on the second evening after my husband's return, I followed him when he attempted to flee to his study after dinner and asked to speak with him.

To save you and Aunt the trouble of guesses and speculation, I shall tell you directly that I have since spent my days meditating on the very great pleasure a simple, honest conversation can bestow to two people as set on misunderstanding each other as my husband and I have previously been. I knew I had married a virtual stranger, but it never occurred to me how much I had allowed my unfavourable first impression of him to affect my later attempts at understanding him. He has certainly not fared much better, with his preconceived notions of the importance of rank and circumstance.

I shall spare you the details of our *tête-à-tête*; suffice it to say that we have decided not to quarrel for the greater share of blame annexed to our current circumstance. We both know that the conduct of neither, if strictly examined, would be irreproachable. More importantly, we would do well to remember that it is not so much our own conduct but the conduct of others that has led us to this situation. We shall harm none more than ourselves if we do not attempt to make the best of an unfortunate happenstance.

There is a great deal of awkwardness to overcome, to be sure, but the future seems far less desolate now than it did even a week ago. Despite his stern, brusque manner and occasional forbidding mien, there is a kindness to the man I married that I am determined to remember whenever I feel cross with him—which I expect shall be often enough! He is an exemplary brother and a generous, kind master. The very fact that he agreed to marry me when Papa asked it of him proves that he is a gentleman. A good man.

On Sunday, we attended services for the first time since my accident and, while I was stared at as much as before, my discomfort was considerably lessened by my husband's remarkably attentive behaviour. Apparently convinced that I would slip and twist my ankle again as soon as I stepped out in the snow, he tucked my hand firmly in the crook of his arm as soon as we left Pemberley's doors and did not release it until we reached our pew.

After the service, instead of rushing me out the church doors as soon as the vicar had said his concluding words, my husband took the time to introduce me to some of his acquaintances. I am sure I could have done without the rather detailed description of Mr Kingston's gout (the discussion with his wife led me to suspect that she is prone to exaggerating his symptoms in the hopes that he will relocate the entire family to Bath—does this remind you of any particular person of our close acquaintance, I wonder?), but I was pleased that my husband made the effort. The vicar and his wife are to dine with us on Friday—our very first dinner guests, if one does not count the colonel. I confess that I am most curious to see how my husband acts in company!

Oh Jane, I have married a stranger...but perhaps I have also married a friend? After all the distress of these past months, the thought feels comforting.

Give my love, etc. to everyone in Gracechurch Street, and do not forget to tell me how Mrs Fletcher replied to Millie's note about the lost stockings—I am quite simply dying to find out!

Affectionately yours,
E.D.

P.S. As I know you and Aunt well enough to surmise that your minds will quickly jump from conciliation to something else entirely, I feel it my duty to disappoint you at once. Nothing of *that* sort has entered our most sensible conversations, and I would be exceedingly surprised if it did.

Pemberley House, February 15, 1812

My dearest Jane,

Aunt has asked me to persuade you to stay at Gracechurch Street for another fortnight at least—she seems quite put out about your plans to return to Longbourn Thursday next. Dutiful niece that I am, I hereby plead with you to think once more about the wisdom of your decision. As I am sure you are aware, Mama, Kitty, and Lydia are in an uproar over the incident with Mr Brown's second eldest—as is the rest of our acquaintance, judging from Charlotte's recent letter. Do you truly want to arrive in the midst of all that commotion?

Charlotte tells me that the whole of Meryton is rife with gossip over what has happened. Mrs Goulding, I am to understand, has *highly trustworthy* sources claiming that one of the officers of the militia is the culprit. Charlotte, ever practical, pointed out that this whole affair is good news for our family, for it means that the events leading to my marriage are no longer the talk of the town. Perhaps it is so; perhaps I should feel pleased to know that Lettice Thompson's flighty tales have been usurped by this new, scandalous turn of events. But I cannot. Surely the girl has acted very, very foolishly, but thinking of the scorn and gossip poor Mr Brown and his family will face makes me feel ill. I am sure that I can never forgive some of our dear friends and kind neighbours for the repugnant way they turned their backs on our family at the first whiff of a scandal. I have told as much to Mama in my latest letter in the hopes that she might curb her enthusiasm over the downfall of the Brown family, but I fear she will think nothing of it.

As I am sure you remember, I received a most mysterious note from Miss Anne de Bourgh some time ago. Curious being that I am, you can guess that I could not go on without finding out whether she was sincere in her congratulations to me. Therefore I sent her a mysterious little note of my own some weeks ago (hidden in a letter from Miss Darcy, of course. As delightful as I found Miss de Bourgh's mother's recent sojourn at Pemberley, I have no wish to repeat the experience, if at all possible). Two days ago, I finally received an answer—such a sweet one that I find it quite likely Miss Darcy has either dictated to her cousin the exact words she should use or else penned the note herself! To be perfectly serious, I confess I am happy that she replied. Should we ever have to pay a visit to Kent, it is comforting to know that at least one person in that county is on my side (although I much assume she would not dare say so to her mother).

The vicar and his wife dined with us yesterday evening. Mrs Reynolds who, thankfully, has recovered from her remarkably insistent cold (my maid let slip that the cook thinks it was none other than her dubious draught that cured Mrs Reynolds—I suspect we have not yet seen the last of that odious mixture!), knew of the vicar's penchant for venison stew, so that is what we served. What Mrs Reynolds did not apparently know, however, was the vicar's wife's penchant for writing poetry.

Oh Jane. By the time dear Mrs Turner reached the thirteenth—and last—stanza of her 'Ode to Hedgehogs,' I did not know which way to look. Miss Darcy was suddenly drawn to inspect the contents of her teacup most thoroughly, and Mrs Annesley seemed to have recovered her interest in murals. Only my husband sat, as imperturbable as ever and, when Mrs Turner was finished with her recital, clapped his hands politely and said, 'I commend you on your excellent use of the iambic pentameter, madam.'

Mrs Turner looked exceedingly pleased with this praise, but my suspicions arose immediately—underneath that sombre exterior, could it be that my husband was hiding a sense of humour? I am determined to investigate the matter further and will report my findings to you as soon as may be.

Apropos my husband, I fear I must close soon, for I have promised to join Miss Darcy and him on a tour of the orangery this afternoon. The sun has been shining these past few days, forcing the snow and ice to slowly give way to spring. Miss Darcy assures me that there is nothing quite as magical as the play of light in the orangery when the sun's rays break through the countless windowpanes. I am glad she has decided to join us to witness this little miracle for, while my husband and I are attempting to understand each other better and avoid useless arguments, I feel more confident of our ability to succeed when there is a third person present.

Do give my love to Uncle and the children, and be sure to tell Aunt that I have done her bidding and tried to convince you to extend your stay. Do take care to consider dear Miss Bingley's feelings in the matter as well! Her health would be put to great peril if her brother decided to take residence at Netherfield again—something I am sure he will consider the moment you decide to return to Longbourn.

Yours ever and ever,

E.D.

Pemberley House, February 19, 1812

My dearest Jane,

How very sly you have been! And, as always, considerably more sensible than any of your silly sisters. I hereby give you my whole-hearted blessing to return to Hertfordshire; do what you can to restore the reputation of our family from the tatters in which I left it. I jest, of course—but it is only because I am so happy that Mr Bingley has declared himself! Oh, how dearly I wish I could be present to witness the expressions of Lettice Thompson and certain other ladies when Mr Bingley returns to Netherfield and resumes his frequent calls to Longbourn.

Mama, of course, will be delighted to parade the news around Meryton. I am sure that Papa, too, will be pleased that at least one of his daughters will be properly courted under the watchful eye of the neighbourhood and shall only give rise to gossip of the very best kind. My dear sister, I am so very, very happy for you! My only regret is that I cannot be there to congratulate you in person.

You have asked me to describe the orangery and I shall try my best, although I fear that my words cannot quite do it justice. My husband tells me it was built nearly a hundred years later than the main house, but it seems like such a natural addition to the scenery that I can easily imagine it has simply grown there over the years, just like the shrubbery and trees surrounding it. Large paned windows made of Dutch glass cover the walls of the building, and even the roof is glazed—an addition commissioned by my husband only three years ago. Inside, the sun's rays play on the leaves of the dormant trees (lemon, lime, orange, and even pomegranate), creating a game of light and shadow just as magical as Miss Darcy promised me. Out of all that is lovely in Pemberley, I believe the graceful, weather-beaten building sheltering the delicate trees from the chill of Derbyshire winter must have the place closest to my heart. Perhaps, sometime in the near future, you might come and see it for yourself.

Speaking of my new sister, would you be very surprised if I told you she never joined us on the trip to the orangery? Another headache, she said, but I am suspicious. Much like Mama's nerves, her headaches seem to have the remarkable ability to appear and disappear at her convenience—or rather, at my inconvenience! I mentioned to her that if the aches persist, we might ask the apothecary to apply leeches to her temples as instructed by Dr Buchan. The manner in which her eyes widened at my quite innocent suggestion leads me to suspect that her head will not trouble her again in the near future.

I must admit that I enjoyed my afternoon in the orangery a great deal, even in Miss Darcy's absence, but it has also left me confused. My husband told me hardly any of the things I expected him to tell me of the place—another man might have prattled on about the cost of the glazing or the size of the chimney-piece inside —and yet he showed me all the things that most endeared it to me. The repairs in one of the windowpanes where a ball had pene-trated the glass after a particularly spirited shot by Colonel Fitzwilliam during a game of cricket many summers ago. A large fern Miss Darcy used to hide behind as a child whenever she was upset with her brother. The spot where my husband's father proposed marriage to his wife.

Oh Jane! Once again, I do not know what to make of my husband. He is not the most talkative of men but, unlike before, I do not feel so oppressed by his silence. He says the thing he means to say and, if there is nothing of substance to add to the matter, he is quiet. In the orangery, he told me his little stories with warmth but no embellishment. When he was done, he stood back quietly and let me explore by myself. He seems to have returned to his old habit of looking at me a great deal but, while I have discarded the idea that he does it to find fault, the meaning behind his expression leaves me puzzled, to say the least. It is an earnest, steadfast gaze, but I often wonder if it is anything other than absence of mind. Perhaps he is just tired of looking at the walls and pleased that he does not have to now that we have agreed to attempt to reconcile our differences?

He seems to seek me out more often, always taking pains to open a conversation on some topic or another instead of just stalking wordlessly as he did when I was confined to my bed. I cannot tell if it is because of necessity or choice that he does these things—a sacrifice to propriety more than a pleasure to himself. Does he truly wish for my company, or does he seek it out of duty? If we are to be friends, I would hope the former to be correct.

As for my own feelings on the matter, I confess that I have put the past behind me far more easily than I would have thought likely. But then, you know I am not formed for misery. A month ago, I did not think it possible to ever befriend my husband— yet now I am determined to do just that. For my sake and his, as well as for the sake of our family, both present and future, I dearly hope I shall succeed.

I shall close now; I am expecting Mrs Kingston and her daughter to call on us this morning and must think of at least two or three good subjects for us to discuss so as to avoid any mentions of Mr Kingston's gout. In the afternoon, I am to visit a few families in Lambton with Miss Darcy—she has promised to give me a tour of the village, and I am determined to finally see every nook and cranny Aunt Gardiner has so fondly described to me.

I hope your journey to Longbourn will be safe and uneventful— but not so much as to bore you quite out of your wits! Do take care to count your stockings when you pack your trunk. Mrs Fletcher may have declared herself the picture of innocence, but I have always suspected her of a great talent for mischief. Do you remember that time she caught me climbing on the fence? I could have fallen and broken my neck for the fright she gave me, and yet she had the audacity to accuse me of trespassing!

Give my love, etc. to everyone in Gracechurch Street before you leave and to everyone at Longbourn as soon as you arrive. Please do not forget to pen me a lengthy letter with all the news from home—at present I hear of nothing but the disgrace that has befallen the poor Brown family.

Yours ever,

E.D.

CHAPTER NINE

———◁◆▷———

Enough

Pemberley House, February 24, 1812

My dearest Jane,

I have received your letter informing me of your safe arrival just in time to relieve my growing anxiety. If the weather there bears any resemblance to the weather here, I expect the roads were not in the best possible condition for your trip, and I confess that I have quite worried for you, dear sister. However, my concerns over your well-being having been allayed, I allowed myself to be excessively diverted by your descriptions of life at Longbourn for the rest of the morning. I hope you are not displeased with me when I tell you that I read the paragraph regarding Mary and Old Spotty aloud to Miss Darcy and Mrs Annesley—I know you did not mean for me to laugh at our poor sister, but I could not help a little giggle. Is it really true she threatened to never leave the house again unless Papa sold the offending hog to Mr Purvis?

Your inquiries about my trip to Lambton were most conveniently timed, as I just this morning received word that my new gown is ready for fitting. On our tour of Lambton, Miss Darcy and I visited the linen-draper and I bought eight yards of lovely white Indian muslin (it was but five shillings a yard—a prodigious bargain of which I am sure Mama would disapprove!) and some blue ribbon with which to trim it. When he heard of my purchases, my husband asked if I would not prefer to do my shopping at the finer warehouses when we return to London. The Elizabeth of *old* might have been offended, but the Elizabeth of *new* simply smiled and told him that if it would ease his mind, I would not wear the gown on Sundays or when we entertain. I have convinced myself that I know enough of him now to understand that he was not trying to admonish me for my country manners, and I could not help but tease him just a little. Who would have guessed that the grave master of Pemberley could blush so prettily?

Yesterday afternoon, he found me in the library and asked if I would like to go for a turn in the gardens with him—a request that I readily agreed to. The sun was shining and the paths were a little muddy where the snow had melted. To my delight, he directed us towards a path that meanders under the branches of the Spanish chestnuts. I have longed to see the dear old trees up close ever since I first laid eyes on them. Unfortunately, it appears that the feeling has not been at all mutual, for we had not been five minutes on the path when suddenly a large lump of heavy, wet snow fell on my head from one of the traitorous trees.

Oh Jane! You can guess what a charming picture I made, snow covering my hat and dripping down my face. As seems to be his habit at my greatest moments of mortification, my husband was quick to come to my aid, producing a handkerchief from his pocket. Unable to help myself, I started laughing as he dabbed my face dry, imagining the picture we must have made, the impeccably groomed gentleman and the disheveled damsel in distress. Then, quite unexpectedly, he laughed too.

I cannot quite put into words what I felt in that moment. Joy, to be sure, for the brief instant of shared amusement. Sadness, because in the months that I have known him, I had never before heard him laugh. A strange feeling of connexion, of togetherness, that quite defies explanation. The moment was gone as soon as it came, replaced by an awkward, uneasy silence so different from the calm quiet that had prevailed when we first set on our walk. Once we returned to the house, he quickly excused himself, distractedly handing me the handkerchief as if I might still have some use for it.

At supper, my husband spoke nothing of what had happened, instead making odd and unconnected remarks on the food that was served, Wellington's campaigns, and even the vicar's new chaise. To be sure, I half expected him to mention Mr Kingston's gouty foot at any moment.

I cannot decide which bothers me more, my husband's strange behaviour since our walk or my inability to put the incident out of my mind. Do write to me, dear sister, as soon as you can—I am in need of your calm and sensible words.

Yours in affection,

E.D.

P.S. Sitting here like a fool of the first order, fiddling with the crumpled handkerchief as if it could provide the answers I long for, I have suddenly realised that it belongs to Miss Darcy. I made it for her when I was confined to my bed—it has her initials, and the blunders in the stitches are quite unmistakable. But what does it signify? Was it something Miss Darcy gave to her brother, or did he take it in secret for some sentimental reason of his own? Perhaps he simply felt an acute need to sneeze and was forced to borrow a handkerchief from his sister because he had none from his negligent wife?

Pemberley House, February 28, 1812

My dearest Jane,

You, better than any other person of my acquaintance, know that I am a true proficient when it comes to finding trouble. When I slipped and stumbled down the steep bank of Mr Thompson's pond straight into the freezing water, I remember thinking it was the worst that could happen. Of course, I was soon proven wrong, for by the time my husband was carrying me home—his fine clothes ruined by mud, and the blood from the wound in my shoulder—the thought of drowning in the pond started to seem like a pleasant prospect when compared to the acute embarrassment of being rescued by none other than the proud Mr Darcy. Then, as is well known to all and sundry, Lettice Thompson decided to teach me that I was wrong, indeed, to think I could not possibly end up in more trouble than I already had. However, not even the machinations of dear Lettice could have prepared me for the *very great peril* in which I now find myself!

Mama once said that my husband was such a disagreeable man it would be quite a misfortune to be liked by him—and I remember agreeing most heartily at the time. In my defence, he had insulted me quite prettily the evening before Mama's declaration and, therefore, deserved a good share of my censure. To my great consternation, it seems now that my sentiments have undergone so material a change since that time that I hardly know what to think of it. I am afraid that if I do not soon recover my senses, I shall end up more silly than Lydia, Kitty, and Mr Collins put together.

Yesterday evening after dinner, we were sitting in the music room, as has often been our habit. Miss Darcy was playing the pianoforte, and Mrs Annesley was sitting by the bow window attending to her correspondence. I was seated on a small settee by the fireplace looking through Miss Darcy's latest fashion plates and trying to determine if I was fashionable enough to survive the scrutiny of the thwarted London matrons and their daughters who, according to Miss Darcy, are sure to descend upon me as soon as we travel there in April.

My husband had gone to his study to settle some matter with Parker, and thus I startled, turning at the sound of his voice pitched so low that I barely heard him. He said nothing out of the common way—he asked if I was planning to purchase more lovely gowns from Lambton—yet I blushed so fiercely, there was no accounting for it. He then sat beside me with a book, and I tried very hard to think of something clever to say in reply to his little joke at my expense but could think of nothing at all. Nothing, Jane! Can you believe it? To think that only four short days ago I callously mocked my husband in my letter to you because he talked about the vicar's new chaise at dinner. Compared to this newly tongue-tied version of myself, he now seems like quite the conversationalist.

If it were only this one occasion, I should not worry so, but there have been several others. This morning at breakfast, resolved to overcome the embarrassment of the evening before, I set myself to think of at least one thing so clever that it would amaze everyone present and be handed down to posterity with all the *éclat* of a proverb. Then my husband looked at me over his newspaper, smiling just so, and I forgot at once what I was going to say. Next, I decided that I should not reach for the skies and determined that instead of one thing very clever, it would be quite enough if I could come up with two things moderately clever before he finished his cup of coffee.

Alas, it was not to be. Just as I had finally come up with something in close resemblance to a witty remark, my husband leaned over to show me something in the paper, brushing my hand as he did so. I much fear that the nervous flutterings I experienced at that moment would have done Mama quite proud. Mortified, I then concluded that I would do well to discard all attempts at being clever and consider myself very lucky if I could think of three things very dull indeed before my husband left the room. But before I had managed to concoct a single platitude, he got up from his chair, looking pleased as Punch for some reason that quite escaped me, bade us good morning, and was out of the door.

Oh Jane! What a wretched goose I am. After these many weeks of trying to assure you and Aunt that my husband does not hold a *tendre* for me, I confess I now find myself very much wishing that he did. Ever since our walk under the chestnut trees, I have thought of little else. I had not expected it, but I see now that I have come to respect my husband more, much more, than any other person of my acquaintance. It is not only respect that I feel for him but something inexplicably more tender. When I am in the same room with him, I feel content and warm. Safe. When I am not, I often find myself occupied with wondering where he is and what he is doing. If I am not in love with him yet, I fear there is a great danger that I soon will be. How am I ever to tell him all this when a simple look from him is enough to render me quite incoherent?

I sincerely recommend addressing your next letter to Bedlam, for that is where my husband is sure to send me if I do not soon recover my wits. Perhaps, if I am very lucky, he will visit me if he ever finds himself in Moorfields on a Tuesday morn.

Your very foolish sister,

E.D.

Pemberley House, March 3, 1812

My dearest Jane,

Thank you for your sweet letter. I am happy to report that I have not been sent to Bedlam and therefore can reply to your missive from the comfort of my own sitting room instead of a cold, damp cell. I was very pleased to hear that the weather has permitted you to spend so many mornings out in the garden—doubly so when I know that you have done so in such excellent company. I am sorry to say that the weather in Derbyshire has not been nearly as fine; we have had such a succession of hail and sleet that outings like yours have been rendered next to impossible. I am not complaining, mind you, for I have come to learn that staying in has its advantages.

Your Mr Bingley (you might think that I should not yet call him that, but I am convinced *he* would not object to my doing so in the least!) once said that he knew not a more awful object than my husband at his own house and of a Sunday evening when he has nothing to do. As much as I hate to disappoint such an agreeable man as Mr Bingley, I give you leave to tell him that he is very, very wrong. But I shall say no more of that, for I am sure that you would not wish for me to bore you with a long and tedious description of a rainy day, a petty argument, and a first kiss shared by a husband and his wife.

Instead I would like to know what you think of this business with Mama and the harp? Papa has sent me a most amusing account of the matter but, due to his fondness for ambiguity, I find it impossible to determine whether he is more diverted or distressed by the entire development. Should I truly worry that Mama plans to approach my husband with the subject when next we meet, or do you think it a passing fancy? While I am sure that a harp would lend a definite air of elegance to a party and render Aunt Philips quite green with envy, I cannot help but wonder if Mama has stopped to consider the fact that simply owning a harp is of very little use if there is no one to play it.

Very well, dear sister, I shall stop teasing you now and admit to it. Even if Mama was planning to request that my husband provide a string quartet to entertain her at breakfast and Catalani to serenade her dinner guests every Friday, I would not much care. These past few days have taught me that there are such extraordinary sources of happiness attached to my situation as Mrs Darcy, even Mama's flighty plans cannot dampen my mood at present.

On Sunday evening, my husband and I were alone in the library— a rare occasion. My husband seemed perfectly calm, sitting in an armchair, seemingly immersed in the volume in his hands, but I could not be calm. Even the steady patter of the rain against the windows seemed to conspire against my peace of mind. I tried one book, then another, only to discard both soon after I had picked them up, feeling far too lightheaded to concentrate on either. By the time that I was browsing the shelves for a third option, I was starting to feel almost aggravated—after all, why should I feel so nervous when my husband simply sat and read, cool as a cucumber, as if nothing at all was amiss?

Climbing up the steps to reach for a copy of Herodotus from an upper shelf, I did not hear him get up from his chair and was nearly startled out of my wits when he suddenly spoke directly below me. Judging from the smug look on his face, I suspect he was rather pleased to have, once again, caught me unawares.

Oh Jane. After days of dancing around him, feeling foolish and unsure of myself, I fear it was all too much for me. Unable to keep calm a moment longer, I let my ire loose on him and said quite a number of things that I might have regretted later—if not for his most unexpected reaction.

At first, he seemed perfectly unrepentant when I accused him of nearly causing me to fall from my precarious position, making a light quip about catching me if there had been need of it. His calm in the face of my ire only served to irritate me more, and I then cried that I was tired of feeling so very jittery and unsettled around him when it was so perfectly obvious that my presence did not disconcert him in the least.

Then—oh, dear sister—something happened that I am sure I shall never forget, even if I live a hundred years. He climbed up the steps, a look in his eyes unlike any I have seen before. Without ceremony, he took my face between his hands, his thumbs caressing my cheeks in a most distracting manner, a single, muttered word escaping his mouth—'enough.' By the time his lips touched mine, I confess that I had quite forgotten how to breathe.

Dear, dear Jane! Will you think me very foolish and improper for the words I have just written? I cannot help it—I feel as if I am the happiest creature in the world. Perhaps other people have said so before, but not one with such justice. Where others only smile, I laugh. It is as if a great burden has been lifted from my shoulders, and I feel lighter than the finest down feather. For the first time since that fateful day in November, I feel utterly at ease. Happiness is within my reach, and I am quite determined to grasp it.

I shall close now and spare the rest of my effusions for later. Do give my love, etc. to everyone at Longbourn and write as soon as you can—even if it is only to tell me you think that I have gone quite mad.

Your very affectionate sister,

E.D.

CHAPTER TEN

Girl Disgraced

An express from Pemberley to Longbourn, March 6, 1812

Dear Jane,

I am sure you will excuse me for the short and incoherent form of this missive—I received yours a little more than an hour ago and have hardly recovered from the shock of it all. Lydia, eloped? With Mr Wickham? How can it have happened? You need not tell me, of course, for I know *exactly* how. It is my fault, all of it. If only I had exposed the whole truth about Mr Wickham to Papa instead of vague warnings about the officers not being suitable company for our sisters!

My husband sits across from me, supposedly composing an express to Papa, but it seems that so far he has spent more time sighing and looking exceedingly gloomy than writing. With every shake of his head and with every furrow of his brow, I can see my power sinking. Why should it not, under such an exhibition of family weakness, such an assurance of the deepest disgrace? How frivolous the letter I sent you on Tuesday now seems.

I should not be burdening you with my selfish concerns, not when I am sure you are already carrying far more than your share of vexations. Dear, dear Jane. How I wish I had the words to comfort you. Perhaps it will cheer you to know that my husband intends to assist in the search for our hare-brained sister. To be sure, he is well-known for his ability to save wayward Bennet ladies from the grips of a scandal, so perhaps all is not yet lost.

I have enclosed a small box of hartshorn for Mama. I thought the knowledge it came from the antlers of the finest deer in Pemberley might enhance its effect on her—and perhaps lessen the attention her nerves require of you. Mrs Reynolds assures me that it once saved Parker from death's door. (He had, apparently, made the mistake of trying to cure a minor headache with a potion manufactured by the cook and later been found quite unconscious in the pantry! How unfortunate that Mr Wickham seems to have escaped any ill effects from the cook's remedies while he lived here, do you not agree?)

I shall close now, for it appears that my husband has finally committed to paper everything he wishes to say to Papa. (What it is, other than his offer of assistance, I hardly dare ask.) Do take care of yourself and remember that you have my love, always.

E.D.

Pemberley House, March 7, 1812

My dearest Jane,

Do you remember how Mrs Hill always used to say that no adversity ever seems quite as daunting once you have slept on it? I always suspected there was not much truth to the matter, and now I am convinced of it. If I was grieved by this business with Lydia yesterday, it is nothing compared to my feelings on the matter this morning.

The succession of hail and sleet has turned into a veritable snow-storm, and very few traces of spring remain. My husband left for London early this morning but, looking out the windows, I hope that he has not travelled far and is well sheltered in some nearby inn even as I write. It seems incomprehensible that only two days ago we were walking these halls, my hand quite inseparable from his, making plans to become the happiest couple in the world. A stolen kiss in the nook at the top of the grand staircase or an exuberant giggle trying the patience of the staid portraits in the gallery now seem like distant dreams, at best.

I have been going through my correspondence from these past weeks and months trying to determine if there was some hint somewhere of Lydia's partiality to Wickham but have found none. She mentioned him twice or thrice in passing before I sent my letter of warning to Papa and, after that, not once. If I made a guess based only on her letters to me, I could have just as soon believed that she had run away with Harriet Wright's Parisian shawl (which, according to Charlotte, did not travel to England in the hands of a dashing smuggler but was acquired from the market-place in Brent Pelham when Harriet last visited her aunt), for she has spoken of it far more often and a great deal more fondly than she ever has of the man she intends to marry.

Oh dear sister, I would not wish to shock you, but I fear for a disaster of even greater proportions than we have thus far imag-ined. A thought has occurred to me so vile I can scarcely put it to words for the fear of its being true. Apart from the missives I received from you, every single letter from Longbourn lately has carried some mention of the disgrace that befell Mr Brown's daughter. Do you suppose it possible that the child is Mr Wickham's?

I have sat here a good half an hour contemplating what I have just written and, the more I think of it, the more afraid I am that it is indeed the truth of what has happened. Dear, foolish Lydia! What is to become of her? A girl disgraced and abandoned by a philandering libertine, or the wife of one? Oh! No, no—every feeling revolts!

I am afraid, dear sister, my gloomy suspicions have made you lose sleep for at least a fortnight, and for that I beg your forgiveness—and recommend that you burn my letter as soon as you have read it. As soon as the weather shows any signs of improvement, I shall send an express to my husband and convey my fears to him as best I can. By the time he reads it, I expect he will wish he had never set foot in Hertfordshire, for such must be the disgrace of perchance having to call a man like Wickham a brother. My husband is a good man, and I am sure he will do what he can to aid our sister—but, selfish being that I am, I cannot but wonder if, no matter how the situation is resolved, Lydia's lapse in judgment will have cost me my happiness.

With a heavy heart, your loving sister,

E.D.

P.S. As I look at the words I have just written, I wonder if I should just burn this letter. Even if my suspicions are true, would you truly wish to hear it? If, in the end, Mr Wickham is to be our brother, what purpose would it serve for you to know about this sad business? I cannot decide.

Pemberley House, March 12, 1812

Dear Jane,

A letter arrived from my husband this morning, telling me that he had arrived to London in relatively good time despite the weather and was setting out to meet Papa and Uncle at Gracechurch

Street. The letter was the epitome of short and formal and, like a fool I am hanging all my hopes on three poor little words that seemed lost amidst their rigid companions—in the beginning of the letter he had named me 'dearest' and at the end he assured me that he was mine always, etc. I am sure he would use the very same phrases even if he were writing to his Great Aunt Agatha, yet I hope against hope that there is more to them than simple politeness and courtesy.

I received your letter yesterday and can only apologise for not penning a reply sooner. I confess that I wrote to you on the seventh, but the letter turned out so horrendously gloomy that I could not sleep at night knowing it waited down the stairs to be posted the next morning. I thus stalked down in the dead of night, retrieved the depressing missive, and tossed it into the nearest fireplace. I advise you not to feel slighted, for it contained nothing but the most wretched musings on the situation of our sister and Mr Wickham and, apart from a short description of the true origins of Harriet Wright's famed Parisian shawl, would only have served to needlessly distress you. (At present, I have decided to tell you nothing more about the shawl, for I am sure that pondering this great mystery will provide you with at least a moment's distraction from what has happened with Lydia!)

I would not worry overmuch about Mama's determination to keep to her rooms—she will have to come down eventually; meanwhile, perhaps her seclusion will offer some much needed rest for you all. It is most convenient that the ladies of the neighbourhood are prevented from meeting her when they come to call, for the less they know about Lydia's situation, the better. I am sure that Mama could not help but divulge every sordid detail were she fit to receive callers. Kitty, I would hope, knows better than to spread her vast knowledge of the affair to our acquaintances, although, in light of recent events, there is reason to question her good sense and discretion. I am of a mind to pen her a long, angry letter, but then I imagine you and Papa have already said your share to her and I would likely have very little to add. I have gone through my correspondence with Lydia trying to ascertain if there are some signs in her letters of her partiality to Mr Wickham but have found none. It seems obvious that she has been far more forthcoming towards Kitty than the rest of us.

Miss Darcy has been quite downcast since she learned of Lydia's plight. She even suggested that what transpired is somehow her fault, but I have determinedly tried to uproot all such thoughts. Braving the inclement weather, we went for a walk yesterday afternoon, and she told me more about her dealings with Mr Wickham. By the time we crossed the bridge over the stream, I was feeling so resentful towards him and his deceitful ways that steam was quite blowing out of my ears. By the time we passed the orangery, both Miss Darcy and I were in tears. By the time we were ambling towards the stables, we were so uniformly desolate and miserable, it was only the appearance of Samuel Reynolds chasing after one of my husband's dogs (which seemed to amuse him and distress the poor hound in equal measures) that helped us up from the depths of despair.

Dear, dear Jane! Let us be brave in the face of this new adversity. We have already weathered one scandal in the past year—surely there is only so much that this new turn of events can add to our notoriety? I know your heart as you know mine, and I worry for the distress the circumstances are causing you. Do not lose hope (yes, this is an order—now despise me if you dare!). However things may unfold, I am convinced that among the three of them, Papa, Uncle, and my husband will find a way to make the best of an unfortunate situation.

Give my love, etc. to Mary, Mama, and Kitty—though I do not mind if you sprinkle Kitty's portion with a bit of reproach. As ever, you are in my thoughts and prayers.

With love, always,

E.D.

Pemberley House, March 16, 1812

My dearest Jane,

How good you are to assure that I have something to laugh at even at a time like this. If only I had been there to witness the turn of Mrs Thompson's countenance when Charlotte told her that there is nothing more scandalous than a young lady who takes delight in spreading malicious gossip about her neighbours. My only regret is that Lettice was not with her mother when she encountered Charlotte. Dear, dear Charlotte!

In Derbyshire, it seems a truth universally acknowledged that visitors abound when you least wish for them. It seems to make little difference to the ladies of the neighbourhood that Miss Darcy and I are not supposed to be at home for visitors and that the weather is exceedingly poor these days—we had four ladies call on us yesterday morning alone. Do you think it possible that they can actually smell a scandal? If so, perhaps I should recommend my husband leave his hounds at home the next time he goes hunting and take Mrs Turner, Mrs Bartlett, Miss Bartlett, and the dowager baroness of Sinclair with him instead. With such an apt sense of smell, they might be of remarkable benefit to the hunting party.

This morning brought only two callers—Mrs Kingston and her eldest daughter—but they were so persistent, I am sure that the effort we extended to entertain them would have sufficed for six or seven visitors of a less persevering nature. They stayed with us for two whole hours, and I was starting to wonder if they were hoping for an invitation to dine with us; Mr Kingston, I hear, has gone to Derby on business, and I can well imagine that a loquacious lady like Mrs Kingston is feeling the shortage of attentive ears around her dinner table keenly.

On any ordinary day, dinner with Mrs and Miss Kingston would have seemed like a pleasant prospect. I do enjoy Mrs Kingston's company, and Miss Kingston—much like Miss Darcy—is a shy, sweet girl. I have tried to encourage my sister to spend more time with her, for I believe they might make great friends—that is, if they ever manage to say two words to each other before Mr

Kingston's gouty foot forces the entire Kingston family to remove to Bath permanently. However, I do not feel I possess the equanimity these days to smile and laugh and discuss the weather over pudding. My thoughts are too full of this business with Lydia to leave room for anything else.

I received a letter from Aunt Gardiner yesterday. As I am sure you already know, it is now absolutely certain that Lydia and Mr Wickham have not gone to Scotland but are staying in some unfortunate corner of London. According to Aunt, my husband has spoken to a lady with some connexion to Mr Wickham, and there is hope that our sister will soon be found. I am relieved to know this, and yet pettily upset that it was through Aunt and not my husband that I heard these things. He does not write. Miss Darcy tried to convince me that I should not read anything into it, but I cannot help it—I worry when I do not hear from him.

At the oddest hours of the day, I find myself feeling angry. With whom, depends on the hour. With myself, often enough, when I think that I could have prevented all this from happening with a single letter explaining Wickham's past dealings. With Mama and Papa, at times, because they did not do more to curtail our sister's wild ways. With my husband, on occasion but never for long, because he does not write. With Lydia and Mr Wickham, all of the time. Their heedless, inconsiderate behaviour has hurt everyone around them. Her youth must be her excuse but, for him, I can offer none.

Do excuse my foul mood, dear sister; I shall try to think of happier thoughts when I next write. If nothing else works, I shall read your delightful description of Mrs Thompson's expression again and again until I have laughed enough to make my stomach hurt.

Please give my love, etc. to everyone at Longbourn, and especially to yourself and a certain gentleman at Netherfield—that he is still there, still by your side despite what I am sure have been numerous demands from his sisters to return to town, has endeared him to me even more, if such a thing is possible.

Yours in affection,

E.D.

P.S. Do take care to tell Mama that a baroness has called on me—perhaps that will keep her thoughts away from the hedgerows?

Pemberley House, March 19, 1812

My dearest Jane,

I am sure your sentiments at the moment bear great resemblance to mine—thank goodness, they have been found! A rider arrived not half an hour ago with an express letter from my husband. Miss Darcy, Mrs Annesley, and I had retired early this evening, and I was already fast asleep when my maid came to wake me. Now, of course, I cannot even think of sleeping.

That Lydia must marry a man like Mr Wickham is undoubtedly a disaster of grand proportions, yet I cannot help but feel relieved. Perhaps they will find a way to be happy in time, despite the inauspicious circumstances that necessitated the marriage. (As you can see, dear sister, I am trying very hard to adopt some of your philosophy—and the effort is making me appreciate your good nature all the more.)

My husband's letter to me, as before, was remarkably succinct. He explained that he had found our sister, and that there was no other recourse but marriage. On the last line of the note, however, hid a most unexpected sentiment—his parting words were that he hoped I might forgive him in time. I am not sure what he wishes me to forgive, for it is certainly not his fault that our sister has thrown herself into the power of Mr Wickham! If arranging a marriage was the only recourse to remedy the situation, it was hardly his doing. I can only hope that he will return home soon so I may find out what he is about—considering his curt and cryptic writing habits, it might take us a decade to sort this matter out through correspondence, and I am far too impatient to wait that long.

Outside, a relentless rain is slowly but steadily sweeping away the last remnants of the snowstorm we had a fortnight ago. The storm looks to have been the last effort of winter to prevail. Spring seems determined to arrive, and I shall happily welcome it. I do not remember ever experiencing another winter quite so cold and erratic in its ways as this one has been. Then again, perhaps it is the unpredictable ebb and flow of my own life that has made it seem so. Do you suppose that for the next one and twenty years we might have nothing but mild weather and placid winds? I am tired of all things tempestuous.

I shall close now and see if sleep finds me. In a few short weeks, we will depart to London—I hope you will consider visiting with us for a good length of time during our stay there. I must admit that I am a little nervous about going to town and can think of nothing that would comfort me better than your presence. More importantly, I miss you dreadfully. How long has it been since we last held hands and shared a laugh? I hardly wish to count.

Give my love, etc. to everyone at home—let us hope Mary has no plans to elope with the vicar's son and that there will be some peace again at Longbourn once Lydia has married.

Your affectionate sister,

E.D.

Pemberley House, March 25, 1812

My dearest Jane,

It is a day for letters—I have received one from you, one from Charlotte, one from Aunt Gardiner, and one from Mama. Sage young lady that I am, I saved yours for the last, and a blessed thing it was that I did, for it provided just the sort of balm one needs in order to rally after reading two full pages of Mama's plans for Lydia's upcoming wedding. Her aim was to assure that my husband and I would arrive to town to host the wedding breakfast

—a notion I am afraid I must disabuse her of as soon as I may. I sincerely doubt my husband will ever allow Mr Wickham to set foot in his home. Even if I thought he might, I am sure I would never ask it of him.

Aunt's letter provoked me almost as much as Mama's—although through no fault of her own. The utter lack of contrition from Lydia and her perfect ingratitude towards the people who have taken such great pains to remedy her situation have made me think that perchance in her, after all, her husband has found his equal. Perhaps each can teach the other something of the evils of selfishness as the primary motive for all actions and, in the end, it will serve to improve their characters?

My husband is to return to Pemberley the day after tomorrow. Determined not to let his terse missives intimidate me, I have penned him a long letter in response to his recent express conveying both my sincere gratitude for his once again performing a great service to our family as well as my hope that he might return to Pemberley sooner rather than later. In reply, we have had another brief express from him informing us there was some dire matter of business he would have to take care of but that he expected to arrive at Pemberley the day after tomorrow, on Good Friday. He had blotted over the last words of the letter—which was surprising, as he is nothing if not fastidious.

To prepare for his return, Miss Darcy, Mrs Annesley, and I have decided that we will do tomorrow everything we had planned to do the day after. That way, we will be able to spend the entire morning of the twenty-seventh looking out the windows for any sign of his carriage and the rest of the day either chatting merrily with him (Miss Darcy and Mrs Annesley) or trying to interpret every move of his head and every twitch of his brow to decide his mood (myself). My wretched heart thumps nervously in anticipation of his arrival, and my head is far too full of foolish thoughts for my liking.

Inspired by Samuel Reynolds, who happened upon me in the park some three days ago, I have (with more than a little help from Mrs

Annesley, I must admit, for my first attempts turned out quite atrocious) embroidered my husband a set of new handkerchiefs that carry his initials and a very clever pattern of two dragonflies below them. I am quite proud of my achievements and hope he will like them—if nothing else, they should save him from the trouble of borrowing handkerchiefs from his sister!

Embroidery, at least, is an art in which I can boast some improvement. Miss Darcy and Mrs Annesley have more than once tried to include me in their pursuits of decorating various objects with filigree, but I confess that I am quite appalling at it—I can roll papers charmingly, but that is as far as my talents go. I am afraid that the very accomplished ladies in town will find me woefully inadequate; they will spend many a spring afternoon in various parlours drinking tea and discussing my husband's odd choice of a wife.

Charlotte's letter contained the news of the Brown family. Were you as astonished as I was? But of course, you must have been, for who could have foreseen such a solution? East Indies! And to think I once thought Derbyshire the end of the world! I had thought that the family's most exotic acquaintance would have been Mrs Brown's relatives in Shropshire, but Charlotte tells me Mr Brown is acquainted with a colonel in His Majesty's Army who has connexions in the East India Company. How extraordinary, do you not agree? But then, to escape a scandal, I am sure the East Indies is just the place to be. It seems unlikely that even the most determined gossips of Meryton could spread the news quite that far. I can only hope the winds are favourable and that the Browns arrive to their destination soon and unharmed.

Equally astounding, I think, is the information I have from Aunt on Mr Wickham's resolution to quit the militia. Aunt tells me it is his intention to go into the regulars once the wedding has taken place. Apparently, he has the promise of an ensigncy in a regiment now quartered in the North. With the number of debts I am sure he has left behind him in every town and every county he has visited of late, I am surprised he still has friends willing to help him with such matters! It all seems so conveniently arranged that I am inclined to think that mischief of the *best* kind is afoot. I have my suspicions on the matter but, since that is all they are as of yet, I shall say no more at present.

I shall close now, for Miss Darcy has come to announce that we are to practice a duet to perform for my husband once he arrives. It is a charming idea, to be sure, and will certainly make *her* talent on the pianoforte appear in the best possible light—I can see myself already, desperately trying to fumble through a piece with some small semblance of grace, my fingers shaking under the unnerving gaze of my husband. How are the mighty fallen!

Give all my love to everyone at Longbourn—someone must have it, if my husband should not.

Affectionately, your most gloomy and rather impatient sister,

E.D.

CHAPTER ELEVEN

—◁◆▷—

Specks of Mud

Pemberley House, March 28, 1812

My dearest Jane,

At length the day is come on which I am to fight my last with my husband. I expect to be well scolded when I tell you this, but it seems that I have worried you with my bleak suspicions for naught. All is well. So very, very well that I hardly know how to put it into words. But for your sake, I shall try. (See, I am vain enough to think that your happiness depends on a thorough knowledge of the trifling minutiae of my life!)

My husband arrived home yesterday afternoon—to our surprise, he came on horseback and arrived at the house so soon after he had been sighted that I barely had time to compose myself. Which was just as well, as there was very little chance of being able to compose myself in any case. Other than his fretful wife, everyone was well prepared for his arrival. The sun was shining, bright and unabashed. The servants stood in line outside the front door, ready to greet him. Even little Samuel Reynolds had made his way to the end of the line, which amused me even in my nervous state, for he was at least two feet shorter than the footman next to him but every bit as grave and solemn.

Miss Darcy was standing next to me, nothing remotely solemn in her appearance, and I must admit that I was envious of her excitement—I was too agitated to feel anything of the sort. I had longed for my husband's return but, when I saw him, my longing swiftly turned into dread. How could I bear it if I had forever lost his affections? But of course, I had lost nothing of the sort and felt remarkably foolish and melodramatic afterwards for ever allowing myself to think so.

When he dismounted his horse, I could naught but look at him. He looked like a man who had travelled quite a distance, to be sure, but so much had I longed to see him that even the specks of mud on his cheek seemed dear to me. But he did not look at me. He nodded to the servants, exchanged a few words with Parker, and kissed his sister's cheek. Only then was it my turn. He seemed to look right past me, mumbling my name by way of greeting, and my chest tightened with disappointment at his cold manner. Then he bent down to kiss my cheek, and I felt his nose brush my cheek, his lips lingering a few moments longer than perhaps was necessary. Just as I thought I might very likely faint like the most missish of misses, he exhaled sharply, as if he had been holding his breath, and quickly stepped back.

Oh Jane! The moment was so fleeting that it might easily have been nothing more than a figment of my imagination. But it was enough—I found myself looking up at his dear face, hoping as I had scarcely allowed myself to hope before. In return, he offered me his hand and I took it, pleased as Punch when he twined his fingers through mine.

When we went inside and Parker offered to take his coat, my husband looked at our hands joined together and said that he had rather keep it on. I daresay Parker looked appalled at the thought of the muddy garment entering any of our finely decorated rooms and, whilst all he *said* was 'very good, sir,' I am sure he did not *think* it a very good plan at all.

Oh dear sister! I jest because I do not know what else to write. How does one put happiness on paper? Is there a word to describe that strange mixture of utter calm and complete unrest that one feels when in the presence of a loved one? If there is, I do not know it!

See, you have caught me. After all these years, your all-knowing sister has finally run out of wit. From now on, my letters shall be equal parts saccharine and trite without a single clever sentence in sight. A few months from now, if you were to compare a letter from me to a letter from our dear cousin Mr Collins, I am sure you could not tell one from the other!

Should I tell you of the very serious conversation we had in my husband's study? Of the awkward moment when we each tried to apologise to the other at once? Like me, he was blaming himself because he had failed to ensure that Mr Wickham did not attempt his old tricks again. Should I try to describe the consummate happiness that overtook me when he knelt in front of me, took my hands in his, and told me that, while our union might not have had the best of starts, for many, many weeks now he had thought of little else than my happiness? Or attempt to make you blush with too many details of the tender kiss that inevitably followed?

Very well, I shall spare your sensibilities and close now; we shall save my meagre efforts of explaining for later. It is as well that I should close, for my husband has awakened and seems to think letter-writing a waste of such a beautiful morning.

He and I have had our share of grievances and petty arguments, and perhaps I did not always love him so well as I do now. But in such cases as these, a good memory is unpardonable. This is the last time I shall ever remember it myself.

I started this year more bitter than I have ever been in my life, my heart full of resentment over what had happened—feeling ill-used by our gossipy friends in general and Lettice Thompson in particular. But from this day forward, I promise never to be bitter again. I have forgiven them all. After all, for what do we live but to make sport for our neighbours, and laugh at them in our turn?

Affectionately, your loving sister,

E.D.

Pemberley House, March 29, 1812

My dearest Aunt,

There is another letter, very much overdue, which I am keen to write today. As I love you infinitely more than the recipient of the other letter, I have decided to first take up my pen and reply to your last. I am sorry I did not do so sooner—but to tell the truth, I was too cross to write. Convinced as I was that my husband had lost his affection for me, I thought that you supposed more than really existed and were too blithe in your treatment of my worries.

Do you remember when I warned you not to draw your assumptions of my husband's character merely based on his handsome looks? How wrong I was, and how right you were! He is as handsome inside as he appears from the outside—perhaps even more so.

Can you imagine that he thought himself in danger of falling in love with me for quite some time even before we were married? He has confessed as much to me, though he also admitted that, at the time, he had little intention of acting upon these feelings. He says it was my fine eyes that first caught his attention. To this discovery, despite his best attempts to ignore them, succeeded some others equally mortifying. During our stay at Netherfield, it seems he was quite desperate to be rid of me—not because he was tired of my impertinence (which he rather gentlemanly likes to refer to as my liveliness of mind), but rather because he was growing too fond of it!

Through these confessions, I have finally come to understand my husband's anger on the night of our wedding. It was certainly not his wish, then, to marry me—but when it seemed there was no other recourse, he resigned himself with considerably more ease than I did. He says he entered the marriage without a doubt of his reception. He thought the benefits of it were all on my side, that I would be pleased and happy, even, by such an unexpectedly fortuitous solution to my problems. What a shock it must have been to discover my true opinion of the development, and on the very night of the wedding. How much he must have regretted then ever agreeing to it!

So very happy as I now am, it frightens me to think of how easily it could all have come to nothing. Had I not stumbled into Mr Thompson's pond, my husband might have left Netherfield—and taken Mr Bingley with him—and who can tell if our paths would ever have crossed again? I did not know my husband then as I know him now, and I daresay that, at the time, I would not have been sorry to see him depart. But now that he is the very dearest being to me in the world, my breath catches in my throat when I think of all the happiness that could have been lost to me.

I want to thank you, dear Aunt, from the very bottom of my heart, for your unfailing support during these past months. What a long and meandering journey it has been to this day—and how very much harder it would have been for me were it not for you and Jane.

I am determined not to think on it any longer, and I hope you shall not either. My union with my husband might not have had the most auspicious of starts, but I am now very much of the opinion that every unpleasant circumstance attending to it ought to be forgotten. This morning at church, the vicar spoke rather eloquently on hope and new beginnings, and I am very much of a mind to agree with him. We should think of the past only as its remembrance gives us pleasure!

At the end of next week, my husband and I are to travel to London together with Miss Darcy and Mrs Annesley. Colonel Fitzwilliam will join us there, to the pleasure of us all. My husband tells me that, during any other year, he and his cousin would have spent this time of spring visiting Lady Catherine de Bourgh in Kent. For some quite unfathomable reason, Lady Catherine has not extended an invitation this year. Most unfortunate, do you not agree?

We are to stay in town for at least two months, perhaps a little longer—it much depends on Jane, Mr Bingley, and the felicitous event we expect to take place in the near future. It is their intention to wait some time to allow the gossip surrounding poor Lydia's wedding to be forgotten (poor Lydia, indeed—or rather, poor Jane, to have such a collection of scandalous sisters!), but I expect the wedding to take place in early June, at the latest.

My husband and I both hope to see as much of you, Uncle, and the children in London as we possibly can—and it will be my great pleasure to introduce you to Miss Darcy, whom I am sure you will come to love as much as I have. If you have not other plans for the summer months, we hope to see you all in Pemberley come July. My husband can introduce Uncle to the best fishing spots on the river while the rest of us explore the park—and do not worry, there will be no need to walk overmuch, as I rather like your idea of ponies. I am determined to invite Jane and Mr Bingley as well—perhaps they would like to use one of the cottages. Would not that be an agreeable prospect? Though I am sure neither would ever say so, I believe they might appreciate some distance after the wedding from both his family and ours.

I shall close now and move on to the second letter of the day, which I expect to be somewhat shorter and rather more formal than this one. It is an overdue note of thanks—to whom, I leave it for you to surmise!

Give all my love, etc. to Uncle and the children—I cannot tell you how happy I am that we will all be together soon!

Your very affectionate niece,

E.D.

EPILOGUE

Pemberley House, March 29, 1812

Dear Miss Thompson,

Do allow me to express my sincere apologies for not penning this missive sooner—I am sure that you have been wondering these many months why I have not thanked you for the fine service you have performed for me. As I know you to be a great advocate of honesty, I feel it my duty to admit I did not at first see your actions in the light I am sure you always meant them. I was resentful, and for that I humbly apologise. I can see now that you were a true friend who only had my very best interest at heart.

I know it will please you exceedingly to hear my husband and I are on the best possible terms and have every plan to become quite the happiest couple in the world. The house and the grounds here at Pemberley are everything that is charming—if so very vast I still must admit to losing my way every now and then—and my new sister, Miss Georgiana Darcy, is a delightful young lady. In a few days, we are to remove to London for the remainder of the Season.

To be quite frank, I did not know such happiness existed. And to think, if it were not for your timely interference, my husband and I might never have married! I shall only add, God bless you, and I hope that you might soon experience similar felicity yourself.

Most sincerely yours, etc.,

Mrs Elizabeth Darcy

P.S. My cousin has a parsonage of no mean size in Hunsford, Kent. He is quite single and unattached. Perhaps, if you ever travel thither, you might make his acquaintance. My venerable aunt, Lady Catherine de Bourgh, resides in close proximity to the parsonage. Like yourself, she is a selfless, unassuming lady who always has the best interest of others at heart—I am sure that you would get along charmingly.

NOTES & REFERENCES

The original text of Jane Austen's *Pride and Prejudice* has been quoted and paraphrased a number of times in the course of this story. These little tidbits I leave for the reader to find—and now despise me if you dare. However, for the benefit of the reader and to give credit where it is due, listed below are some other notes and references that might be of interest or amusement when reading the correspondence of our heroine.

December 25, 1811 (Prologue)

The last line of Elizabeth's letter to Jane is a reference to the last chapter of *Mansfield Park*, in which a very different feeling is expressed by the narrator: *Let other pens dwell on guilt and misery.*

November 1, 1811

In a letter to her aunt, Elizabeth describes her father's enthusiasm towards a copy of *Meditations* her uncle has procured, including marginalia by Coleridge. (The) *Meditations* is a series of personal writings by Roman Emperor Marcus Aurelius, first translated into English in the 1700s. English poet Samuel Taylor Coleridge is known for his extensive habit of writing comments regarding the books he read, ranging from notes of a single word to expansive essays (a habit not uncommon during the era—some examples exist of even Jane Austen doing this). Such notes were not limited to private use and were often written for the benefit of friends, acquaintances, or even a wider audience—or, in some cases, a lover.

Bugle beads, along with ribbon, were a popular trim in the Regency period, even though Elizabeth declares to detest them. In an undated letter from 1811 to her sister Cassandra, Jane Austen reports having worn a bugle-band as a headdress to match the border of her gown.

November 26, 1811

The *Great Chinese Pagoda*, which little Edward Gardiner was determined to climb, was designed by Sir William Chambers and completed in 1762 as a gift to Princess Augusta, the founder of the botanic gardens at Kew. It offered one of the first bird's-eye views of London. The Pagoda was open to the public on Sundays for a small compliment to the attendant.

January 2, 1812

Elizabeth tells Jane that she is *half agony, half hope* when it comes to meeting Miss Darcy. The expression has been borrowed from Captain Wentworth's eloquent letter to Anne Elliot in *Persuasion*.

January 4, 1812

In her letter to Jane, Elizabeth paraphrases Lady Caroline Lamb, an aristocrat and novelist, also known for her affair with Lord Byron, whom she famously described as *mad, bad and dangerous to know*.

January 15, 1812

When Elizabeth first encounters Mrs Reynolds's grandson Mr Samuel Reynolds, he is said to be lurking about the *piano nobile*. It is an Italian term, translating to 'noble floor,' used to refer to the principal floor of a house.

January 19, 1812

Late in January, Elizabeth is nursing a sprained ankle and a severely bruised *amour propre* after an unfortunate encounter with the slippery surface of a frozen pond on Pemberley's grounds. Amour propre refers to a pride or self-love that depends on the opinions of other people. It is a central term in the philosophy of Rousseau introduced in the 1700s.

While injured, Elizabeth hopes that Jane will find time to write to her between endless rounds of *spillikins* with their young cousins. Spillikins is a children's game, also known as pick-a-stick. Jane Austen owned a spillikins set which, in a letter to her sister Cassandra dated on February 8, 1807, she considered 'a very valuable part of our Household furniture.'

January 25, 1812

Crossing, which Elizabeth finds out can be a dangerous occupation while writing on a tottering bed tray, refers to the Regency habit of first writing a sheet full and then turning it sideways to continue writing on top of the original lines to save space. The postage depended on the size of the letter and was paid by the recipient— to keep the letters affordable, it was common to write on a single sheet that was then folded and sealed for sending.

January 27, 1812

In Sermon XIII of *Sermons to Young Women*, Fordyce recommends that 'like the apostles and first Christians, your highest glory is to conquer with benignity, and *triumph by patience.'* Should you ever feel the need to channel your inner Mr Collins, I recommend looking up *Fordyce's Sermons* online—in addition to this sample, the book includes plenty of other charming advice for young women.

Snap-dragon is a parlour game that was popular in wintertime during the Regency era, particularly on Christmas Eve and Twelfth Night. It involved plucking raisins out of a bowl of flaming brandy and trying to eat them without getting burned.

February 4, 1812

Elizabeth refers to a snowball fight between Mr Bingley and little Edward Gardiner. The weather of this story is purely fictional, but it is a fact that winters in the early 1800s were often somewhat colder than they are now; for instance, in the winter of 1814, it was so cold that the Thames froze sufficiently to hold a winter fair on the ice, and there were reports of roads being closed due to heavy snowfall even as south as Kent.

Hester Chapone, whose letters Elizabeth catches Miss Darcy perusing, was a self-educated writer of conduct books for women associated with the Blue Stocking Society founded in the early 1750s by Elizabeth Montagu. Her *Letters on the Improvement of the Mind, Addressed to a Young Lady* (1773) was singled out by Mary Wollstonecraft as one of the few self-improvement books deserving of praise.

February 19, 1812

Elizabeth reports shocking Miss Darcy with the suggestion of applying leeches to her temples to cure her repeated headaches, as instructed by *Dr Buchan*. In addition to the use of leeches for headaches, Dr William Buchan's *Domestic Medicine* (1790) offers plenty of other lovely and practical tips for treating all manners of diseases.

February 24, 1812

After a trip to Lambton, Elizabeth writes Jane that she has bought eight yards of lovely, white *Indian muslin* for but five shillings a yard. This is a reference to a scene from *Northanger Abbey*, where Mr Henry Tilney recounts a story of buying a gown of 'a true Indian muslin' for his sister and paying only five shillings a yard for it, assuring Catherine Morland and Mrs Allen that it was considered a prodigious bargain by every lady who saw it.

February 28, 1812

A tongue-tied Elizabeth describes to Jane her attempts to come up with *one thing very clever, two things moderately clever* or *three things very dull indeed* before her husband quits the breakfast parlour. In *Emma*, during the picnic at Box Hill, Frank Churchill proposes that, as entertainment, the members of the party must offer either one thing very clever, be it prose or verse, original or repeated—or two things moderately clever—or three things very dull indeed, and promises Emma will engage to laugh heartily at them all.

At the end of the same letter, Elizabeth fears that her husband will send her to *Bedlam* and hopes that he should visit her if he ever finds himself in Moorfields on a Tuesday morning. Bedlam (Bethlem Royal Hospital) was a psychiatric hospital/asylum, visits to which were a disturbingly popular pastime in the eighteenth and early nineteenth century. In 1814 alone, there were ninety-six thousand such visits made. Entry cost a penny, apart from Tuesdays, when one could peek into the cells of the patients for free. Bedlam has moved several times since it was opened, but from 1675 to 1815, it was situated in Moorfields, just outside London city limits.

March 3, 1812

Wondering on her mother's insistence on buying a harp, Elizabeth jests that Mrs Bennet might next ask Mr Darcy to hire *Catalani* to sing to her dinner guests. Angelica Catalani was a famed—for her flighty temper and high fees, as well as her voice—Italian opera singer performing at the King's Theatre in London during the time period of this story.

March 6, 1812

Hartshorn, which Elizabeth sends to her distressed mother, refers to the scrapings of the horn or antler of red deer (hart) containing ammonia which (powdered or distilled) was carried in decorative little bottles or perforated silver boxes and used as a smelling salt for fainting spells.

March 7, 1812

A large-scale embargo, starting from 1806 and ending in 1814 after Napoleon's first abdication, with the aim of preventing all trade with Britain and continental Europe, was an essential part of French foreign policy during the Napoleonic Wars. The embargo, largely made ineffective by industrious smugglers and the fact that Britain held naval dominance, had consequences far more weighty than the fact that *Miss Harriet Wright* was unlikely to own an actual *Parisian shawl*.

Discussing Lydia's disgrace, Elizabeth is paraphrasing Emma's feelings on the idea of Miss Fairfax becoming the mistress of Donwell Abbey—*every feeling revolts*.

March 25, 1812

Decorating objects with paper *filigree* was a common pastime in the Regency era. In *Sense and Sensibility* during an evening at

Barton Bark, Elinor Dashwood aids Lucy Steele in making a paper filigree basket to Annamaria Middleton.

March 28, 1812

The first line of Elizabeth's letter is a reference to Jane Austen's letter to her sister Cassandra, dated January 14, 1796: 'At length the Day is come on which I am to flirt my last with Tom Lefroy, and when you receive this it will be over—My tears flow as I write, at the melancholy idea.'

ACKNOWLEDGMENTS

While short, this little story is the work of many years, and I couldn't have done it without the enduring support of the Austenesque community.

Firstly, I wish to thank Jan Ashton and Amy D'Orazio and everyone else at Quills & Quartos Publishing for inviting me to publish my first book, for enticing me back to writing Austenesque after a long, long break, and for supporting me throughout the process.

I owe a deep debt of gratitude to Marcelle Wong, my editor extraordinaire, to my copy editor Debbie Brown, and to Gayle Mills, whose help and support was essential to me when I first published the shorter, original version of this story online in 2011.

I wish to thank the wonderful community of Janeites at A Happy Assembly and in other forums for offering me their encouragement and friendship over the years – and a place to share my love of all things Jane Austen. The fun, inspiration and education I have acquired through reading, writing and talking Austenesque is beyond indispensable. Thank you!

ABOUT THE AUTHOR

Anniina Sjöblom lives in the beautiful but cold Finland and works in university administration. She has an MA in History and enjoys a long-standing love affair with the works of Jane Austen.

When not writing, Anniina spends her time hanging out with friends, binge-watching TV dramas and re-reading her favourite books while the stack of new ones still waiting to be read piles higher on her nightstand. She can ride a unicycle, and once, after losing an unfortunate bet, ate a bowl of ice cream with green dish soap as dressing. She does not recommend attempting it to anyone.

Her previous works include titles such as Thirteen Days, Fix You and When He Comes Back, published in various online Austenesque forums under the pen name boogima. The new novella Thaw, expanded from the original version of the story first published online in 2011, is her first commercially published work.

For more information about Anniina's future publications as well as those of other great authors, please visit www. QuillsandQuartos.com

f facebook.com/AnniinaSjoblomAuthor

g goodreads.com/anniinasjoblom

Printed in Great Britain
by Amazon